Tattoos and Wedding Blues

JENNIE L. MORRIS

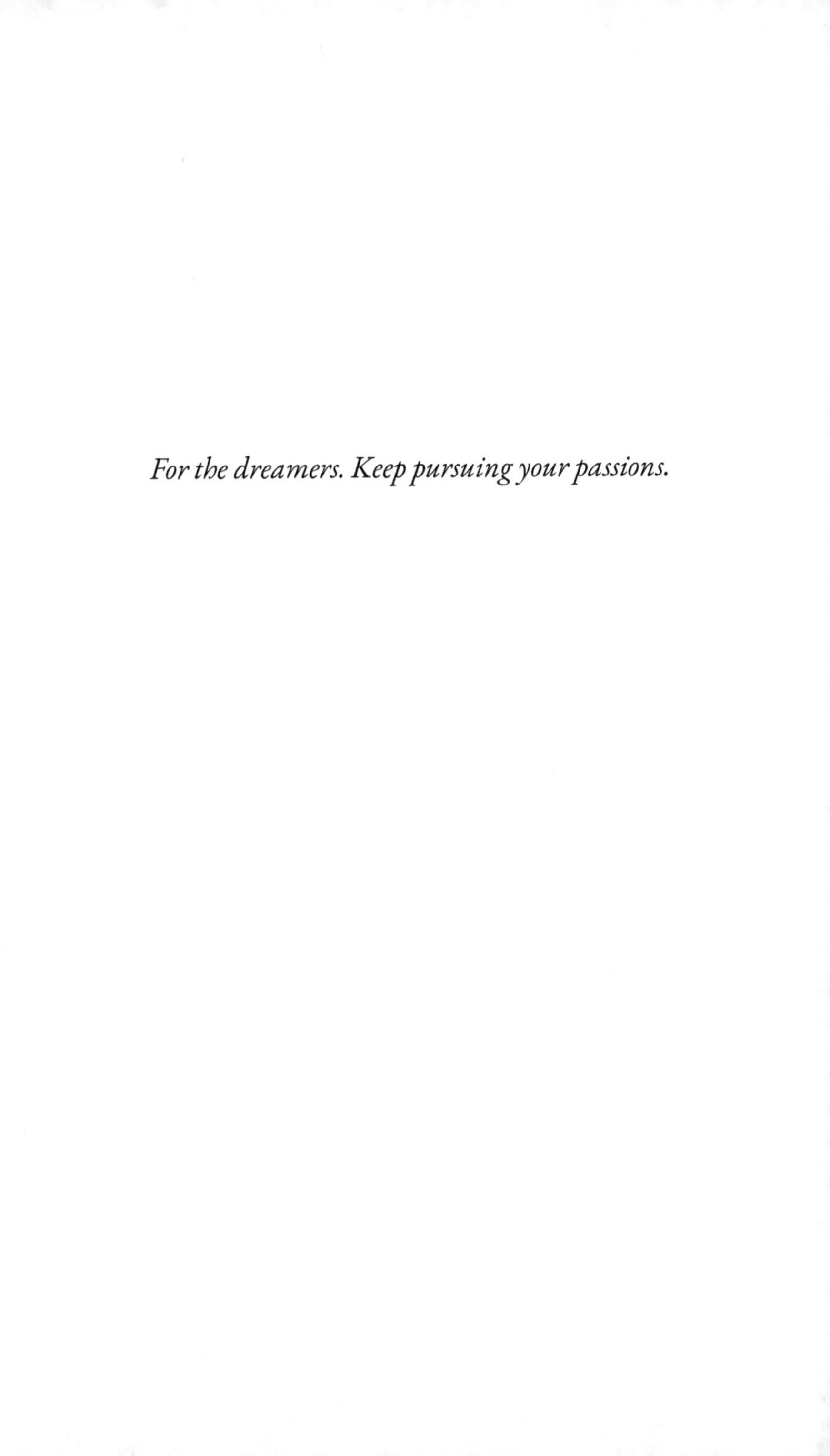

For the dreamers. Keep pursuing your passions.

By all means, marry. If you get a good wife, you'll
become happy; if you get a bad one, you'll
become a philosopher.

— SOCRATES

Lydia

INK AND BLOOD. THE TWO SCENTS ENVELOPED Lydia as she tapped the tattoo machine's foot pedal, controlling the needle's rate. The metal grip vibrated in her left hand like a frightened mouse. She hummed to the punk rock piping through the shop's sound system, a shanty by Flogging Molly, one of her favorites. With a damp towelette, she dabbed away the bright neon blue ink, revealing the gradient shading in the koi pond design.

"How you feeling, Rat? We're almost finished," she said, rubbing ointment onto his long, shaved calf. The tattoo wrapped around his lower leg, covering an old, faded burn scar.

"I'm fine, honey." Rat lay on his side, scrolling social media on his phone. His red bandana covered his graying blond hair tied back in a low ponytail. The battered leather vest, covered in various weathered patches, fit loose against his thin frame. "Did I show you pics of Evie's latest recital?" Shifting his shoulder, he showed a dozen or so pictures of his grinning granddaughter in a sparkling pink tutu with a flower bouquet.

Lydia smiled. "She looks like her pawpaw."

"Just as ornery too." Rat beamed, revealing a gold front tooth. "She told me to get a unicorn tattoo, and I admit, I considered it. My wife would've killed me."

"Unicorns are popular right now." She concentrated on the expanding ripples around a lily pad. "Maybe you and Shayla can get matching temporary tattoos as a compromise. I think Tammy will be okay with that idea."

The man laughed, resting his head on his bent arm. "Are you still doing face painting at the church's art fair?"

"Ah, yeah, I should be there Sunday afternoon. I've got a wedding tomorrow, but Miah'll be at our booth." She glanced at the vintage Kit-Cat Klock on the wall. "Not too much more. We should finish up the next session. Check it out."

Using the antique floor-length mirror, Rat twisted his leg back and forth. He bent forward to inspect the colorwork. "Shoo, you can't even see the scar no more. It's like I got a new leg."

The shop manager, and Lydia's mentor, Di, appeared in the open doorway. "Heya Rat. How's our girl doing?"

"I'd say hire her already, but you know I'm biased." He showed off his lower leg, pointing out where the curve of the koi's back and lily pad covered the worst of the scarring. "Been a long time. I've wanted that gone."

Di crouched, inspecting the tattoo with her reading glasses on. "Good shading, especially around the lily. And you're finishing the koi next?"

"He's still contemplating the pattern," Lydia replied, unwrapping a sterile gauze bandage. "It's between a *Hikari Moyo* or the *Kin Gin Rin*."

"The what?" Di asked, standing. Wearing a monochrome black palette, the lean woman looked ready to lead a congregation in morning prayer. Her shocking white hair, natural, not dyed, added to her austere appearance.

Rat took out his phone, almost an extension of his hand. "Tammy has five koi, and we're trying to pick the colors. She's the fish expert, not me. I'm just the canvas."

Smirking, Di patted him on the back. "Good luck. Wives aren't easy to please." She turned to Lydia. "Catch me upfront when you're done, alright?"

"Will do. Hop up on here, Rat, and I'll get it wrapped up so you can be on your way." She patted the padded black bench. After spraying his calf with green soap, a special antiseptic mix, Lydia spread on a thin layer of ointment and placed the sterile pad on the tattoo. "Schedule the last visit in a month, and we'll get this beauty finished."

"I'm not gonna miss that scar, I'll tell you. Who wants the constant reminder of getting blown up?" Rat pulled out his wallet. "How much I owe you?"

"We've been over it. This is a freebie." Lydia rolled up the used ink pods into the paper towel and tossed the bundle in a biohazard bag. "You're helping me out, remember? This is part of my apprenticeship."

"Honey, I got to pay you something. This is too good. I don't care if it's helping you out; you're putting in a lot of work on this old man's leg." He laid out a hundred-dollar bill. "See you at church. I'm sure Tammy'll text you later."

"I'm gonna get you back!" Lydia called as Rat left the room. A hundred dollars went a long way towards bills, and though she loved tattooing, being an apprentice was an expensive endeavor.

After cleaning and sterilizing the room, Lydia brought her tools to the communal prep station in the back. Using the self-sealing bags, she put the needles in the half-empty autoclave. She tidied the space, putting away clutter on the counters and emptying the trash can. During her apprenticeship, she was the shop's in-house maid. Not a big deal. Before signing up, she knew what the gig entailed, and she enjoyed cleaning. Working at The Illustrated Woman was phenomenal and an excellent place to cut her teeth in the business.

Lydia collected the trash and went out back to the dumpster. Mid-September twilight cast a gloom on the parking lot. Summer heat clung to the air, and she swatted away an unlucky mosquito. Close to downtown Lexington, the main roads had a steady stream of traffic. Located in a strip of retail shops, the tattoo parlor was prime access for the university kids, business types, and soccer moms.

Di sat behind the check-in desk, doodling in her massive art book. "Grab a seat," she said, without glancing up.

Being twenty minutes to closing time, the shop's front room was empty of waiting clients. Lydia went behind the desk and sat in the soft, padded armchair. The Illustrated Woman showcased Victorian décor: dark emerald velvet couches, replica damask wallpaper, authentic cameo portraits in oval walnut frames. A rose and lavender candle burned on the vintage handmade display case, giving the area an aged ambiance.

Sipping from her tea-stained mug, Di leaned back in her swiveled chair. Lydia eyed the sketch: a tattoo design of a laughing skull with wilting roses.

Di grabbed a yellow legal pad. "How long have you been working here?"

"Close to a year," Lydia answered, her hand brushing the corduroy-like fabric of the armrest. "I think I started October eighth, officially."

"A year, already?" She shook her head. "Damn, I'm getting old. Don't tell Marian. She's on this 'fifties is the new thirties' kick. I hate to break it to her, but we're not thirty."

"I mean, she's stunning. I'd kill for her genes." Lydia adored Di's wife, Marian. "Sign me up for her skin-care regime."

As if summoned by the conversation, Marian entered the shop with a glow of a confident woman. She wore shorts and a t-shirt sporting her yoga studio's logo.

Somehow her messy bun looked perfect, as usual. "Slow night?" she asked, hoisting up her oversized designer bag.

"The boys are finishing up," Di replied. "How was class?"

Marian crossed her arms and leaned on the display case, separating the desk from the seating area. "Good. Beginner classes are my favorite. Everyone's all legs and elbows, no ego." She motioned for Di's cup. "This better be decaf."

"It's not alcohol. Does that count?"

"You're insufferable." Marian gulped down the last of the tea. "Are you ready, sugar-tits? It's your turn to make dinner, and I want something other than takeout."

"Give me five, and I'll meet you in the car," she said, blowing her wife a kiss. "Sorry about that, Lydia. Can we continue this—when are you back in the shop?"

"Monday morning."

"Perfect. First thing on Monday, we'll have this chat." She shoved her art book into her tote bag and swung it over her arm. "By the way, good work on Rat's tattoo. Scar-tissue can be fiddly. I'm gonna see the boys off and head out. Have a good weekend."

Lydia waved. "Stay safe out there."

LANDING ON THEIR LUMPY COUCH, LYDIA sighed and took off her worn-out Chuck Taylors. She stretched out her legs, noticing her mismatched socks.

She considered going to bed without dinner, again. It was too much of a hassle.

"You're home late," Miah said, coming from her bedroom. Dressed in cartoon pajamas, her half-sister looked twelve. "Want me to make you a sandwich?"

"Would you?" she asked. "I'm beat."

In their kitchenette, Miah grabbed cold cuts and cheese from the fridge. "Wanna know a secret?"

Lydia suppressed a yawn. "Hit me, sis."

"They're looking for a replacement at work, full-time. Gio put my name in for the position."

"Yes!" she cheered, clapping her hands. "About time. I knew I liked Gio. He's a good egg."

Carrying a plate and a glass of water, Miah walked into the living room and sat on the couch. She pursed her lips in thought. "What does that even mean, 'a good egg?' It's so weird."

Lydia bit into the sandwich and shrugged. "What do I look like? A college professor? It's just something people say."

"Do they? Maybe in the 1950s."

"Stop! Tell me about this promotion, or whatever," she said with a mouthful of food. "Are we talking about a raise? Benefits?"

"I think so. I'll be eligible for benefits, at least." She rubbed her face. "What a relief, huh? No more paying full price for my meds. Maybe we can look for a better apartment, you know, not so close to the strip clubs. Don't get me wrong, those women got skills...but we live in a shitty neighborhood. I'd like a little more trees and fewer liquor stores."

Snorting, Lydia slapped at her sister. "Our mamas worked at one of those."

"And?"

"You're too much tonight. Did you get into the booze, or what?" She swallowed the last bite of the sandwich and washed it down with the lukewarm tap water. "I hope you get the job, and not for the insurance, but because you deserve it. I mean, insurance is helpful, but we're managing."

Less than a year apart, the sisters shared everything—besides looks. Each took after their respective mothers' sides of the family. Miah possessed a flawless copper complexion, golden hazel eyes, and a ready smile. She was tall, close to five-ten, with voluptuous curves. Short, maybe five-three, Lydia was pale, with stormy gray eyes and blonde curls. Well, pink and blonde curls at the moment.

Miah adjusted her satin sleeping cap. "Managing? When's the last time you had a day off? When's the last time you bought a new pair of shoes? And Goodwill doesn't count."

"It's called being environmentally conscious. Look it up."

"It's called being broke," she retorted.

Calling a truce, Lydia held up her hands. "Better than living at home, right? Thanks for dinner. I'm calling it.

Got a big wedding tomorrow, so I won't see you until late."

Waving her hand in dismissal, Miah sauntered to the kitchenette. "If you get a chance, bring me home a piece of cake."

Aurelius

"Perfect, hold right there...and great, thank you, everyone." Aurelius lowered the camera and blinked his tired eyes. "Looks like that's it. I've got a wedding in—an hour. Don't want to be late."

The boys ran off the football field, shouting and swinging helmets at one another in a strange game where only the players knew the rules. Their parents chatted in groups of threes and fours, oblivious to or ignoring the chaos of energetic middle schoolers.

Rolling his shoulders, Aurelius lifted the worn leather camera strap from his neck and went for its case. He grabbed a bottle of water and swigged, feeling a migraine creeping around his temple to his left eye socket.

"Thanks, A. I appreciate it," said Jordan, toting a torn mesh bag of footballs. "I know this isn't your usual thing."

"It's been a while, but a photoshoot is a photoshoot," he replied, slinging several gear bags over his shoulder. "Can't let our alma mater down, can I?"

"Coach Jordan!" shouted a boy with shoulder-length green hair. "My mom wants to know when we'll get the pictures?"

Aurelius rubbed his pulsating temple with his fingers. "Two weeks? Three? Tell them three."

A short, loud conversation passed between the coach and concerned parents. Jordan waved to his team, telling them to go to the locker room. "Are you sure you can't stay? We've got a game this afternoon."

"I wish. But this," he raised the camera bag, "pays the bills. I'm headed home to change. I'll call when I've got the edited proofs." He had ideas for tweaking the shoot. By using a few preset filters in his software, he planned to give the photos a professional ad campaign look. No way he'd let those boys down; they'd be the best-looking team in the state.

"Alright, man. We'll grab a beer, maybe go to a UK game like old times. My treat," Jordan offered, shaking his hand. "Don't be a stranger."

After agreeing to a free meal and game, Aurelius headed to the parking lot. With all his gear settled in his jeep, he drove the fifteen minutes to his townhouse. Along the way, he called his assistant, who was at the wedding location. Cyndi gave him a run-down of the basic layout and potential shoot areas. They couldn't access the house to scout potential spots beforehand as it was a private residence. As his eyes and ears on the ground, she played a vital role in reading the event's atmosphere. So far, she rated it at DEFCON Three.

From his spare room's closet, he selected a gray three-piece suit, fresh from the dry-cleaners, and a pair of polished black oxfords. Before hopping in the shower, he popped his migraine meds. A late-summer wedding, swarming with high-profile guests, needy parents, and a demanding couple while dealing with a pounding brain, sounded intolerable.

Showered and dressed, Aurelius sprayed on citrus-based cologne and left his half-empty bedroom. In the expansive kitchen, he grabbed another dose of migraine meds and shoved them in his breast pocket. He glanced at the two magazines on the granite counter and snagged them. He left with keys and knock-off aviator sunglasses in hand.

First, he punched the address into his GPS. Driving southwest, he left Lexington and followed the busy highway. The city receded, and rural pastoral homesteads dotted roadsides. Horse Country. Multi-million dollar stables housed potential derby winners. Long stretches of centuries-old limestone rock fences followed old property lines, bulging under the pressure of time or the slow growth of trees.

A Lexington native, Aurelius spent his childhood in his parents' authentic Greek restaurant. The Montanaris were transplants from New Jersey. In an effort to fit in, they held annual Kentucky Derby parties and talked about the University of Kentucky's basketball as if it were a religion. However, the family had no interest in anything outside the city. Aurelius was a bona fide urbanite.

The roadway narrowed into a one-lane route. He maneuvered the jeep around a steep curve, tires hugging the pavement when the house came into view. It was a legitimate mansion. Old money. A true remnant of Antebellum South.

At the gated entrance, a security guard in full uniform stopped him. The man checked his ID against a list and then waved him through. Aurelius followed the wide drive lined by towering oaks. "Jesus, I'm visiting Tara," he mumbled.

He saw Cyndi waiting near a sign for valet parking. She wore her black designer dress, a staple for these events, with sky-high heels and a bright blue scarf around her neck. Her cinnamon brown hair was pulled back in a French twist. He could tell she was tense by how she gripped her paper coffee cup.

Aurelius parked his jeep and handed his keys to the valet driver. Going to the back, he went to grab his gear. "Hey, Cyndi. Have you finished the bride's boudoir shoot?"

"No," she stated, tapping her foot on the pristine brick sidewalk. "She's adamant you take the photos."

Slinging the bags for his two DSLR cameras, attachments, and his favorite analog camera onto his shoulder, he frowned. "How *adamant* is adamant? Like, she's throwing a minor fit...or I'm going to have to remind them of the signed contract?"

Cyndi motioned for the bag with the foldable tripod and footstool. "Immovable. If you're going to insist on the contract, you're going to have more than an unhappy bride on your hands. Her mother and father want the best for their baby's first wedding." Her lips puckered, perturbed about the situation.

He understood her chagrin. Cyndi was an excellent photographer and more than qualified to handle a few sexy photos. In fact, he hired a woman assistant primarily for the intimate bridal pictures. Aurelius had nothing against nudity; it was part of the job, but working with professionals was one thing—handling brides was another. Women tended to be more comfortable with another woman behind the camera. As a bonus, it freed him up from any sticky situation with jealous grooms.

"Fine," Aurelius conceded. "Tell them I'll be up." Before shutting the back door, he grabbed the magazines and handed them to her. "The interviews. Tell me what you think."

"You haven't read them?" she asked, tucking the high-end bridal magazines under her arm.

He shook his head. "I'm not going to either. Give me the highlights when you've got time."

Laughing at his discomfort, a soft, comforting sound, Cyndi headed up the brick walkway to the arched double-door entrance to the house. Aurelius went the opposite direction, following the signs to the reception area in the backyard.

Manicured flower gardens hugged the stone exterior of the mansion. Real wood shutters, painted a pristine white, graced each window. He leaned back, trying to count the floors. Four? Five? Someone added to the original house. The expansion doubled the building's size. He liked the fairytale-like pepperpot turret, with its stained glass window and climbing ivy.

A mammoth white tent housed dozens of round tables in the sprawling back lawn. The florists, caterers, servers, and band prepped the area for the post-nuptial party. The wedding planner directed a horde of workers in white shirts and black pants as they flittered from table to table, smoothing out pressed linen table clothes, fixing the fine china, and setting out cut-crystal glassware.

He retrieved his camera reserved for outside venues, already set up with the right lens and lens hood. With the aging summer sunlight and deep shadows, he went through the aperture settings, snapping several test shots until he liked the results. From his spot, by an impressive rose of Sharon, he spied several potential locations for intimate photos for the couple.

Readying to go into the house, he overheard a heated discussion. A young woman in a server's uniform and a lady in an oversized two-piece suit stood a distance from the tent, their body language defensive. Half the conversation melded into the background noise at that distance, but he got the gist: the older professional disliked the young woman's pink hair.

Not that it mattered, but he found her bubblegum pink hair cute. It complimented her rosy complexion. Having no dog in that fight, he sighed and prepared for his own battle.

* * *

BIANCA BARDOTTE CINCHED HER RED SATIN robe tighter, accentuating her narrow waist. Her parents, Earl and Lindsey Bardotte, conspired by the enormous window framed by lush blue velvet drapes. Aurelius wanted to walk out the door, hop into his jeep, and call the whole thing off. The money was nice, but he would return the deposit if it meant he was free and clear of the situation—and the Bardottes.

"Does this room have enough lighting?" Bianca asked, reaching for one of the ornate columns of the king-sized poster bed. "The Princess room faces north. Would that be better?" She batted her enormous false lashes, or she had something in her eye; he wasn't sure which.

"Ah, no, this is fine." Stalling, Aurelius rechecked his light meter. Agreeing to do the boudoir shots was one thing, but asking for sexy poses in—well, whatever she wore underneath the robe in front of her parents was two steps beyond uncomfortable. "I'm almost set, but I must insist. This is a closed shoot. You and me."

Mrs. Bardotte stepped forward. A ready protest jumped on her plump lips. "And I must insist we stay. We won't be in the way, will we, Earl?"

"Dear, really, I—"

"See, it's settled. We'll stand right here by the window. Won't say a word," she continued in condescending placation, as if she won the argument.

Struggling to hold his tongue, Aurelius rubbed his left temple. The dull thud of his migraine threatened to explode into a full-on episode. "Mrs. Bardotte, they need you and your husband for the wedding party photos. Cyndi is coordinating with them as we speak." He wasn't sure if this was true, and he didn't care. "Since we switched roles, a concession despite our signed contract, I recommend you take the win and head downstairs."

Mrs. Bardotte squinted. "We're paying your exorbitant fee, and you dare speak to me with that tone."

"Mom," interrupted Bianca, stepping in between the two parties. She flashed Aurelius an apologetic smile as if that made up for everything. Maybe in her world, it did. Rich, beautiful people got away with ridiculous behavior. "He's not wrong. You didn't read the contract. I did. He can, technically, leave, and we'll owe him the entire sum." She guided her parents to the door. "What are wedding party photos without you and daddy? Mr. Montanari is a professional. Murphy and I trust him."

Giving them a gentle shove, Bianca pushed her parents out into the hallway and turned the door's lock, guaranteeing privacy. With the elder Badrottes gone, she offered him a lengthy apology. She leaned against the door frame, playing with a tendril of her tousled ash brown hair. Teetering on mile-high stilettos, she bit her pouty lower lip.

"Do you forgive me, Mr. Montanari?"

Turning his back to her, Aurelius pretended to examine the room. "I don't follow, Miss Bardotte."

He heard her move across the wood floor to the bed. The duvet gave a soft whisper of fabric brushing fabric when she sat down. "For breaking part of the contract."

"Ah," he stammered, "call it a onetime thing. Cyndi said you were insistent."

"Though I deal with property acquisitions, I'm well aware of the legal repercussions for pressing this matter," she continued. "It's just, this sounds a little pathetic, but I saw your campaign for Sweet Treats a few years back, and I've been somewhat obsessed with your work since then."

"That was, let me think, five years ago. One of my first big jobs." He screwed on an additional light to his camera. "People aren't interested in the photographer at lingerie shops."

"I think I bought nearly every piece in the collection that season. You made those women look sexy. I mean, of course, they're sexy but also powerful. Like they own Fortune 500 companies or climb mountains or hunt lions."

When Bianca paused, he turned to look at her. She

shrugged, tossing her hair over her shoulder, and said, "I want to kill lions."

He thought she was kidding until he caught her dead gaze. He wondered if the groom knew he was marrying into a psycho family or was he going in blind. "Why don't we start with you by the window, and we'll work our way to the bed," he suggested, hearing a squeak of awkwardness in his voice. "Take advantage of sunlight."

She stood and untied the robe as if undressing for a lover. Beneath it Bianca wore a black and white lacy teddy, with sheer cups and thong undies. He ignored her perky, too-perfect breasts and her dusky pink nipples.

After several minutes, Aurelius had a strange inkling Bianca wasn't a novice. She required little prompting, and her poses were far from amateur. The entire session lasted fifteen minutes. He snapped over a hundred photos and expected most of them to be high quality, something quite unusual for a blushing bride during her first and probably only risqué photoshoot.

Bianca replaced her robe and laid a hand on his forearm. "Thank you, Mr. Montanari. That was perfect."

When he went to reply, she put her finger to his lips and shook her head. She left the room. Her rose and tobacco perfume lingered.

Lydia

"I CAN'T UN-DYE MY HAIR, MS. BARRA," LYDIA explained in sincere confusion. "I'll have to get the color stripped out by a professional." She wore her hair pulled up in a high ponytail. It was neat and tidy, as required. That morning, the staffing company owner, Mr. Barra, mentioned the pink ombre was 'fun' when he handed out their paychecks.

"No one gave you permission to add that ridiculous color. It's a distraction and unprofessional. Are you trying to make the company look bad? Are you trying to make *me* look bad? We hired you with all *those things* on your arms, and you go and do this!" Ms. Barra tugged at her oversized suit jacket's hem, a nervous habit. Her outfit was two decades outdated and not in a flattering, quirky way some people could pull off. The dress suit was boxy, muddy brown, with shoulder pads and enormous gold buttons. It did nothing for the woman's rounded figure.

Frowning, she crossed her arms, self-conscious of her tattoo sleeves covered by her white dress shirt. "Of course not, Ms. Barra. I love working for Barra Hospitality. My friend needed practice for her cosmetology class, and I offered. I guess I didn't think it would be an issue since Brian has blue highlights. It was at the last minute. She had an exam and...."

As soon as she mentioned Brian, Lydia regretted it. Her supervisor's pinched expression transitioned to real anger. "This conversation doesn't concern Brian. You need to worry about yourself and not your co-workers. Cover up that color, or I'm going to have to send you home without pay."

"But I've already worked three hours—"

"You heard me," Mrs. Barra interrupted, smug with her ounce of power. "If I don't see that covered up, you're going home."

Defeated, Lydia replied, "Yes, ma'am." Bowing her head, she slumped away. She couldn't afford to lose the job, not yet, not without a contract with the tattoo studio.

Under the tent, setting out the expensive china plates, her friend Ras watched her weave through the tables. A considerable flirt, he was a hit at weddings, always ready with a compliment. He had dark eyes, tan skin, and luscious black hair worn in waves to his collar. On a slow night, he left with half a dozen phone numbers. It was too bad for the ladies; he was in a steady relationship with a charming man named Greg.

"What did *The Leech* want?" Ras asked as he shined a butter knife with a clean towel.

Self-conscious, she reached up to her ponytail. "My hair. I've got to cover the color, or she's sending me home. Do you have any bobby pins?"

"For God's sake!" He threw down the towel on the table, the butter knife skittering across place settings, clanking against china dinner plates, and landed on the grass. "I swear, if she'd pulled those damn granny panties out of her crack, she might be tolerable. What about Brian?" Bold as a glitter bomb, Ras pointed at the man across the tent.

Handsome, in a sleazy white-trash sort of way, Brian stood chatting with Kayla. He leaned against a wooden fold-out chair, examining the end of his black tie. The aqua blue highlights glowed in his blonde hair, taunting Lydia.

A master at manipulating vulnerable people, Brian showered them with fake compliments. He cultivated phony friendships because they served a purpose. Lydia liked Kayla, but she was under Brian's spell, his number one fan and defender. Ras called her his work bitch, without benefits

"I brought it up, but you know how it goes. Brian can do no wrong." She patted her pockets in vain. No bobby pins. She knew that already, but it was worth checking.

Huffing, Ras scanned the tent. "They should do the nasty already. All their eye-humping grosses me out."

"Please, stop." No one needed the image of Brian and Ms. Barra partaking in horizontal refreshments.

He cracked a grin. "Brian and Barra sitting in a tree, F-U-C—"

"I may throw up." Lydia picked up the towel and tossed it at his face. "Cover for me while I go find the hairstylists. Maybe they'll have something."

Smirking, Ras nodded, pretending to dab his forehead and cheeks with the towel. "I'll just do all the work, shall I? Go on, little miss thang, get your hair did, so we can get paid. Leave this old maid here to suffer in the southern summer heat alone."

Lydia blew him a kiss, amused by his theatrics. She jogged across the lawn, sidestepping her hustling coworkers as she made her way to the colossal house. Of all the events they outfitted, she liked outdoor weddings the best, even in the heat.

The property had multiple buildings and an acre-sized pond. The various sized buildings were in excellent condition. Lydia guessed a few were originals from the 1800s. When she arrived, she saw a placard stating the property was on the registration of historical places. It was likely an old plantation, renovated and modernized.

Down a long drive, in the distance, were the new stables. Far enough away to keep any unwanted smells at bay, but close enough, the owners can show off their prized horses. She suspected they owned other animals, too. Lydia didn't consider them livestock, like on a working farm or ranch, more like family pets or hobby animals. She'd heard a distant goat's bleat or a dog barking throughout the day.

Lydia skirted by the glamorous wedding party as they clustered under a weeping willow's graceful green bows. The photographer, a woman with a commanding presence, gave directions to the garrulous bridesmaids. She teetered on a small plastic stool wobbling on the uneven grass.

"Flower girl. Yes, you, I need you to move in just an inch. Okay, and bridesmaid on the far left, can we turn the shoulder in? Perfect." She lowered the camera, sighing. "Someone needs to fan out the skirts. No, not you."

Slowing her stride, Lydia waved her hand. "Can I help?"

"Would you? That would be great," the photographer replied. "I need their dresses draped on the ground."

One by one, Lydia spread out the women's pale blush gowns, listening to the photographer's directions. She moved aside when everything was in place, pleased by the scene. The bride's party smiled, holding their bouquets, stunning against the verdant green backdrop.

The photographer stepped down from the stool, adjusted something on the camera, and circled the group, getting shots of different angles. When she passed Lydia, she thanked her, never looking up from the camera's viewfinder.

With her one good deed done for the day, Lydia

rerouted back to the house. She fell in line with a group using the side door, bypassing the grandiose family entranceway. Using the direct route to the kitchen, she saw the catering company set up in stations in the cavernous room. They wore pristine white smocks and frittered over cutting boards, ovens, and stovetops, while one woman shouted out orders—a shepherdess leading her flock of skilled sheep.

She'd worked for Barra Hospitality for three years, serving at weddings, corporate events, reunions, birthday parties, and the occasional funeral. It was common to run events with a handful of the same caterers. The Lexington/Louisville area was small, and it was hard to break into the business of gaining old money's trust. Lydia couldn't recall working with this company before. She saw no familiar people in the kitchen.

"French," said Kayla, carrying a stack of linens.

"French what?" Lydia asked as she stepped against the wall, leaving room in the hall for people to pass.

Kayla joined her, arms folded over the fabric to keep them in place. "The caterers are French. Flown in for the wedding. And I guess the small pre-wedding party last night, but we didn't get that booking."

"That's something new. Not the booking part, but the French part," she stumbled. "Don't rich people fly over to have destination weddings, not bring the destination to them?"

"Right?" She adjusted her arms, the bulky table linens cumbersome to hold. "I think it's one of the grandparents. They're ill or something, so they planned the wedding here. I overheard Ms. Barra and Brian a few days ago. Sorta sweet, redoing the whole thing for your granny."

Lydia agreed; it was a nice sentiment. And she wasn't at all surprised Kayla eavesdropped on Brian's conversation. "Do you know where they're doing hair and make-up?" Shrugging, Kayla pointed up. "My guess too. I'll be right out to help with the tables." Not waiting for a reply, she pushed on down the hall and ascended the first stair-case she saw.

Determined to complete the annoying task, Lydia curbed the urge to explore. The house held gorgeous antiques mixed with modern elegance. One of the groom's aunts, a knock-out in a cream and navy sheathe dress, directed her to the correct floor.

To give freedom to the bridal party and female guests needed hair or makeup, they cordoned an entire wing of the fourth floor off. A warning sign forbade men. Lydia heard high-pitched laugher echoing down the dark-paneled hall and figured she was in the right place.

At an open doorway, she peeked inside. Three women sat on cushioned chairs wearing robes over their fine outfits. Makeup artists hovered over them, applying layers of product like delicate paint, building up their masterpiece on their living canvas.

"Hey there, bride or groom?" asked a curvy woman with a cheetah smock. She poured champagne into fluted glasses and handed them out. "Honey, you in the door-way. Are you with the bride or groom?"

Giving a nervous laugh, Lydia stepped into the room. It smelled of sticky hairspray and hot curling irons, of sweet perfume and talc. She imagined this was the smell of a theatre's dressing room.

"Neither, ma'am. I need a few bobby pins. My boss wants me to put my hair up," she said, searching the various workstations for the allusive pins.

"Take a seat." The woman pointed to an empty chair. "I'll be right over."

Afraid to decline the offer, she sat and crossed her heels. Another round of laughter came from the women. They were older, perhaps in their late fifties, and obviously close family or friends. Lydia overheard bits and pieces of the conversation, something to do with a boy and summer.

The hairdresser returned, wiping her hands on a towel. "So, what do you need again, honey?"

"I'm with the serving staff. My boss wants to send me home if I don't cover up the pink."

"Have they never heard of self-expression?" She clucked and got out a comb from a pocket on her smock. "Maybe a sock bun. The ombre goes high. We might not get all the color, but we'll try." Brushing out the few snarls in Lydia's ponytail, she pursed her lips. "What salon did you get this done at?"

"None," she answered, meeting the woman's scruti-nizing gaze. "My friend's enrolled in a cosmetology program. I was her victim. Is it bad? You can tell me, I'll give her pointers, she'll appreciate it. I think it looked nice, but I'm not an expert or anything."

She lifted a lock into the air, pointing out the delicate gradient of blonde to bright pink. "Your friend did this at her house?"

"Yes, ma'am."

Letting go of her hair, she dug around her workstation and then went to a roll-away case tucked by the wall. "Here we are." She held out a business card to Lydia. "Tell your friend to call me when she finishes her program."

Lydia looked over the card. She'd heard of the salon. It was some place downtown, too rich for her blood. "I will. Ah—" Giving a smile, the woman tapped the name on the bottom of the card with her fingernail. "Nateesh."

"The one and only, honey," Nateesh said.

Swift and talkative, Nateesh reminded Lydia of Miah's mom. She liked to stay busy, always in motion, either talking or smoking or bouncing her foot. It'd been a while since she visited with Angel. She got in bad with a druggie boyfriend a year ago, and it wasn't the same visiting their house. To stay sober, Lydia set boundaries, and keeping away from users was at the top of the list.

In less than five minutes, Nateesh fixed Lydia's hair problem. She primped, tucking the pink strands under with pins. As she suspected, some color showed at the bun's base. Using sprigs of flowers meant for the wedding, Nateesh added a few stems, secured them in place, and sprayed on one additional layer of hairspray for luck.

"No one will ever know," she said, holding up a mirror.

Amazed, Lydia covered her open mouth. Her hair was etheric, something right out of a Victorian photograph hanging in the tattoo parlor. "Wow, this is, I feel like I'm going to prom or something." She fished in her pocket, going for the small wallet she carried while working. "I have to pay you. This is too nice."

Nateesh put her hand on Lydia's shoulder. "Honey, it's on the house, or the Bardotte's check, really. They paid by the hour, not the client."

Reacting, she hugged the woman. "Thank you. That's really nice. And it's hard to find nice people."

"Been one of those days, hasn't it? We've all been there." As if on cue, the makeup artists looked up and nodded in agreement. The women in the chairs were oblivious to the side conversation, drinking champagne, lost in their reminiscing. "Keep your head up, Lydia. This is only temporary, right? We've all had shitty days and shitty bosses. Go flirt a little, make some boy smile. That'll help you forget about it."

"Nateesh!" howled one of the makeup artists. "You bad! Don't listen to her, Lydia. She'll get you into trouble."

"Maybe that's what she needs, a bit of the right kind of trouble?" Slapping her hands, Nateesh coaxed her hips into a low dipping circle. "Nothing wrong with it, am I right, ladies?"

Flaming red with embarrassment, Lydia covered her cheeks but grinned. "I wish I could stay! You all are too much, and I love it."

Nateesh lifted her arms in the air and snapped her fingers, dancing to a song only she heard. Lydia left the room to high-pitched whistles. She waved her hand at her fiery face, chuckling. All she wanted was to get through the rest of the day and go home. Flirting was not on the agenda, neither was trouble-making.

Not paying attention, on the staircase landing, Lydia collided with someone. She dropped to her knee, clutching her left shoulder. The sudden aching feeling was familiar. She had a bad habit of stumbling into walls and doorframes, moving through life unaware of her surrounding. Klutz, her, no way.

"Are you alright?" asked a man, offering his hand.

Rubbing her tingling shoulder, she nodded. "Yeah. I'm sorry, I wasn't paying attention." She stood, not taking his hand on purpose. It felt weird and intimate.

"No, it was me. I was staring at this, and I didn't see you." He held up an expensive camera, sheepish in his admission. His tailored gray suit enhanced his warm, dark features. A trimmed black beard covered his angular jaw, and his soft rounded eyebrows gave him an open, receptive appearance. "Are you with the wedding?"

"The wedding?" Lydia blinked. Was he joking? She couldn't tell. She blended in with the other serving staff, wearing her flattering non-slip black shoes, black dress pants, white button-up shirt, and tie. No one confused them for wedding guests. She dared to look up, seeing a mixture of amusement and bewilderment. "The wedding! Oh no, I'm not here—" she waved her hands in a circle, indicating the fourth floor, "—for wedding stuff. I need help with something. I'm with Barra Hospitality."

He removed the camera strap from around his neck and tucked the camera in his arm like a football player securing the ball, ready for disaster to strike without warning. "I just thought, with the hair, you might be someone. I mean, you are someone, obviously." He stopped and ran a hand over the back of his neck. "I'm Aurelius, the photographer."

"Lydia," she replied, relieved he was just as discombobulated as herself. "Not to sound sexist, or whatever the term is now, *genderist* maybe, I don't know, but I thought the photographer was a woman."

"You mean Cyndi Postman. She's a talented photographer and my right hand." The sound of approaching footsteps on the stairs drew his attention.

Frowning, the woman Lydia saw by the willow tree ascended the staircase, her eyes set on Aurelius. When seeing them alone on the landing, her lips pressed into a flat line. "Now I see why you're not answering your texts."

"I should go," Lydia stated, holding up her hands, hoping to stave off any potential confrontation.

"Don't let me interrupt." Cyndi directed her

deadpan delivery to Aurelius, ignoring Lydia. She shifted on her heels, her designer dress molded to her hips. Compared to the tall, refined woman, Lydia blushed at her frumpiness. Funny, minutes ago, she almost thought herself pretty. What a blow to her ego.

The mounting tension overwhelmed the narrow corridor. Lydia inhaled and clapped her hands together. Maybe today was not the day to put Nateesh's advice into practice after all. "I do have to get back. It was nice meeting both of you. Best of luck with the photos. I'm sure they'll turn out great."

She caught an apologetic look from Aurelius as she turned for the stairs.

Aurelius

THE PRICKLING HEAT OF THE AFTERNOON dampened his collar as he crept around the crowded seating area. Eager family and friends waited for the wedding to begin as the sun beat down, breaking through the trees' shade. Aurelius snapped candid photos of the groom and his men, chatting in hushed tones, elbowing each other far too often. The Catholic priest in his ornate robes gripped the make-shift pulpit, eyeing the bartenders mixing cocktails and icing bottles of imported beer.

Me too, buddy, he thought, wishing he had an Old Fashioned or four. His migraine was in full swing after the confrontation with Cyndi. Maybe confrontation was too harsh. No...no, it was definitely something. She got into moods sometimes, but who didn't? He could be a real jackass; it happened.

The incident by the staircase was reactive, like a boss

catching an employee slacking on the job one too many times. He shrugged it off and decided to talk to her later. Weddings were tense, and the high-profile event added another stressful element.

On the tail of two national bridal magazine interviews, this was a critical time for both their careers. Aurelius agreed to the brutal dissection of his process with the stipulation the magazines included a section showcasing Cyndi and her work. Maybe that was a bad idea to do without warning her first, but he saw it as an opportunity to drop her name to potential clients.

Melodic chords struck up from the band, announcing the bridesmaids. Putting his eye to the viewfinder, he transfixed on minute details: the sheen on the pink champagne dresses, the curl of the carmine rose petals, the elegant curve of feminine necks.

The wedding planner gave Aurelius a breakdown of the ceremony in advance. He stationed himself in optimal positions to get the best angles while remaining courteous to the guests. Whatever shots he missed, he expected Cyndi to pick up the slack. It was common to have several thousand images to filter through for these big events.

Snap. Snap. Snap.

"By the power vested in me by the Commonwealth of Kentucky, I now pronounce you husband and wife. Son, you may kiss your bride." The priest beamed, his jolly, rosy cheeks the epitome of ecclesiastical perfection.

"May I be the first to introduce Mister and Missus Murphy Kendricks."

A thousand butterflies filled the air as the couple filed down the aisle. Their soft, downy wings fluttered and swooped skyward, creating a fairytale moment. The insect cloud awed. It conjured delight in young and old.

Aurelius paused, amazed. What couldn't money buy? He checked his watch as an usher released rows to join the growing queue of well-wishers. He had twenty minutes, maybe twenty-five, while the guests clamored through the receiving line. Taking a moment, he went to the open bar, needing a nip to get through the next hour.

"What can I get you?" asked the bartender, rubbing a towel on the clean work surface. She dressed in all black, her dark hair pulled back into a severe bun.

"An Old Fashioned, please."

He watched the bartender's deft fingers pour in bitters, a dash of water, and drop in a sugar cube into a rocks glass. After muddling the ingredients, she uncorked a fine nine-year bourbon and added the warm amber liquid. Finishing the drink, she twisted an orange peel over the top and dropped a round ice cube into the glass.

Aurelius thanked her, lifted the drink to his lips, and shoved a tip into the half-empty jar. The bourbon coated his tongue and warmed his throat. He limited his alcohol to a glass of wine or champagne to toast the couple. Today was an exception.

"Getting soused already? A bit unprofessional." Cyndi ordered tonic water with a splash of lime.

Ignoring her attempt at a joke, he gulped down the Old Fashioned. "I think I can handle it."

"Are you going to stay pissy?"

Eyeing her, he turned and pressed his back against the bar. The wedding planner and her team had an efficient system to move guests from one area to another. Servers carried silver trays of hors d'oeuvre as the band played elevator-style music.

"Why don't you grab the rest of the detail pics and move onto the reception? I'll finish the groups." He finished the drink and set the glass in an empty gray tube used for bussing tables. "I want out of here as soon as possible."

Cyndi blocked him from leaving. Her manicured hand pressed into his chest. "You said I could do the couple's shots."

"I did, but I've changed my mind," he replied, side-stepping her.

"So, you're punishing me? For what? Calling it how I see it."

Biting back an instant retort, he closed the distance between them. "This isn't a punishment, Cyndi. This is a judgment call. I don't know what's going on up here," he said, pointing at her forehead. "But you're distracted. Think about what you said for a moment. We're adults, and yes, I'm technically your boss, but I'm your mentor first. It's not my job to dole out punishments.

"However," he continued, noting her anger at her dressing down, "your snarky, belittling remarks are neither helpful nor warranted. Gear up, get out there and let's finish this event. We can continue this conversation later."

* * *

Using the app on his phone, Aurelius updated the master shot list. He finished the group portraits with a modicum of sanity remaining. Mrs. Bardotte hovered like an opinionated house fly. Her buzzing comments distracted him. He swatted at his ear multiple times to drive her voice away.

The candid couple's photos went smoother. Forced to oversee the party, Mrs. Bardotte left her post, accompanied by a swarm of well-meaning family and friends. Aurelius relaxed, rolled his tense shoulders, and did his best to brush off the mounting annoyance.

Bianca and Murphy took directions well. In their designer wedding attire, they looked like models for a bridal campaign. Like many grooms, Murphy left most of the planning to his bride and the mothers. Aurelius knew next to nothing about him. The longer they worked together, he realized Bianca was the personality of the couple. Not to say Murphy was a dullard. He was pretty on the eyes but as personable as a cardboard box.

Using the late afternoon light to frame solo photos, Aurelius zoned out. He concentrated on the golden glow around Bianca's curled hair, the sunlit veil, the shine on her red lipstick. Lighting was vital, and he preferred natural to artificial lamps. These were some of the best shots of the day.

"So, you live in Lexington?" Murphy asked and then slurped on a canned hard seltzer.

Hiding his aggravation, Aurelius answered, "Since grade school."

"Cool, cool. It's alright, for what it is. Got to go to the big cities for the good stuff, but it's decent," he continued.

What did he mean by *the good stuff*? Aurelius doubted it was cultural experiences. "I wouldn't really know."

"Bro. You have to visit Europe. The ladies, you know, they like Paris and Milan or whatever for the shopping, which is fine. But the parties. Ibiza is dope. Like, twenty-four-seven, party until you can't remember your name, insane. Berlin, Jesus, Berlin. Those Germans can throw back." His excitement was akin to a child getting ice cream at a baseball game. "We should hang sometimes. You look like you can throw back. And Bianca thinks you're hot."

Aurelius fumbled with the camera. It slipped from his grip, saved by the neck strap. "What?"

"Is something wrong?" Bianca called. She shielded her eyes with her bouquet.

Murphy downed another swig of his drink and wiped his mouth on the back of his hand. "I told bro here you thought he was hot and that he should hang."

"So direct," she chuckled, blowing her husband a

kiss. Then, as if enacting a business transaction, her mien changed. "He's not lying, Mr. Montanari. I hoped we could speak to you privately. Murphy's enthusiasm is appreciated, but he can be too eager."

Waggling his eyebrows, Murphy threw his arm around Aurelius's shoulder. "I love when a woman talks business, don't you?"

"Sure," Aurelius said in confusion. He shifted his attention between husband and wife. What just happened? They smiled in encouragement, expecting something from him. Rubbing his temple, he relented in the awkward stalemate. "I'm sorry, I've missed something."

Moistening her lips, Bianca closed the distance between them. She ran her hand along Murphy's arm and interlaced their fingers. "You're adorable." With her free hand, she fingered his lapel. "We want to get to know you better. Maybe see where things go if you're interested."

"A Devil's threesome can be like taboo, or whatever, but we're all about respect and fun for everyone involved." Murphy squeezed his arm, tightening his grip on Aurelius's shoulder.

All the bits and pieces clicked into place. Married a few hours, and the Kendricks already sought a third person to join in their bedroom play. Aurelius flushed with heat, flattered by their proposal, but intelligent enough to decline the offer. He tried a threesome once. It was a fiasco of arms and legs, ending with his girlfriend dumping him. She started dating the other girl. He heard they moved to France a few years ago for their clothing line.

Forcing the nervous laugh aside, he put a hand in his pocket to hide the white knuckles. "What a compliment, coming from you both. I'm not against consensual adult fun or anything, but I had an unpleasant experience with a multi-partner rendezvous. It turned out not to be my thing."

"Oh, what a shame." Bianca pouted and tugged on his lapel. "The right couple makes all the difference." Bold as brass tacks, she pulled him to her, pressed her cheek to his, and inhaled. "You do smell nice. I thought you would."

Watching Murphy watch them, Aurelius felt dirty. The man's mouth parted, and lust gave his eyes a hazy heaviness. Aurelius was an afterthought at that moment, a plaything for the couple to fixate their passions on. The sexual tension rose. Any second, they would rip their clothes off and make the beast with two backs on the lawn. Wouldn't those pictures look great above the mantle?

Bianca stepped back, tossing her hair behind her shoulder, laughing. "That's hilarious, Mr. Montanari."

Marching like the captain of an armed regiment, the wedding planner advanced, her strict schedule in hand. On the best occasions, the planners were a necessary evil. Today, he wanted to buy her the MVP trophy for saving his ass. "Everything's set for the big entrance, love birds.

Have you got everything you need?" She directed her question to him.

"I believe so." He checked his camera settings to avoid eye contact.

"Perfect. Everyone's waiting."

The trio left, a bubble of animated conversation surrounding them.

Relieved, Aurelius grabbed his hips and exhaled. He turned his back to the party and cursed. Decision time. He planned on changing the website as soon as he got home tonight. No more wedding bookings. He loathed weddings.

And he needed a drink.

Lydia

"THESE ARE GOURMET?" LYDIA ASKED RAS AS they loaded up on the next serving trays for the cocktail hour. Decorated with little Washi-tape pendants, the long wooden toothpick pierced the petite triangles of bread and gooey cheese with a roasted heirloom cherry tomato on top. "It's a fancy grilled cheese sandwich. Not even a sandwich, more like a grilled cheese bite."

Ras grabbed one and tried it. "Tastes alright. My grandma's grilled cheese is better, though."

Snorting, she covered her mouth and scanned the bustling kitchen for spying eyes. "You're going to get us in trouble."

"Only if The Leech sees us. She should be at least five drinks in, undressing Brian with those bloodshot eyes, wondering if he's wearing whitey-tighties or boxers." He put his hand over his heart, his recent manicure of gold and pearl tips fitting for the occasion. "Girl, that boy wears them whitey-tighties two-sizes too small. Thinks it accentuates his lower man bun."

"I don't want to know." She coughed on her spit. Picturing Brian at all went too far. "Wait, how do you know what he wears?"

He raised his left eyebrow, giving a sinister grin. "I've seen things."

Too close to the occupied tent to continue the juicy conversation, Lydia mouthed, *"This isn't over."* As a prelude to the five-course dinner, she wandered through the mingling guests as they imbibed in custom cocktails and nibbled on canapés. She half-listened to their discussions, paying attention to her fellow servers. Multitasking was essential when doing these gigs.

The crew at Barra Hospitality had an in-house form of sign language. It was similar to cheating at cards but not as thrilling. The signals helped avoid particular pitfalls commonplace in the service industry and helped the company garner its stellar reputation. Guests came in various flavors: sweet, sour, and some plain disgusting. If someone came across a handsy perv, woman or man, they rubbed their nose. A picky guest—pull on the earlobe. It wasn't complicated, but Ms. Barra often confused the gestures, to their amusement.

"Hey there," said a man as he plucked a sandwich from her tray. Flipping his wrist, as if by accident, he flashed his diamond-studded cufflinks. "These any good?"

"I expect so, sir," she replied, putting on her best company smile. No one wanted a grumpy server.

Clamping his perfect teeth on the toothpick, he slid the food off in a single bite. He chewed, nodding his head. "Decent enough, I guess."

"Good to hear, sir. I'll let the catering company know your thoughts. Would you care for another?" She put the tray between them with its three remaining hors d'oeuvres. On the outside, he had the makings of a catch—the clothes, the looks, the cologne—but his almost frat-boy mannerism crawled up her spine. Hoping she misjudge his character, she added, "If you want more, I can go back to the kitchen."

He licked his full lips with their seductive cupid's bow. "I'd like to get your number instead," he replied, staring right into her eyes as he licked his finger. "Or maybe we can go somewhere private."

Ah, there it was. He didn't disappoint. Weddings brought out some real winners. What was it about an overpriced bouquet and a dry cake that switched off people's manners? Rude was rude, no matter the setting.

Holding her smile, Lydia adjusted her tie. She should walk away, pretend she heard someone calling her name, anything to get her away from him. "And where would we go?" The words slipped out on their own. His interest piqued. She clucked her tongue; why hadn't she kept her mouth closed? Now she was in it.

"We can find an empty room." He stepped forward, shoving the tray's edge into her chest. The metal pinched her skin, and she winced. Romeo was oblivious to her discomfort and growing aggravation, preoccupied with thoughts of scoring tail. Lydia took a half-step back, bumping hard into a table. The glasses rattled. Reacting, she checked to see anything got knocked over. While she was distracted, his hand slid between them, and he settled his hand high on her thigh, his fingers inching upward.

On instinct, Lydia reached forward and grabbed his testicles. She squeezed, gritting her teeth together. All reason left her head, and in its place, red hot anger told her to tighten her grip. *Make him suffer.* She and Miah grew up with bullies. They survived a rough neighborhood and a run-down high school. The women at the strip clubs taught them how to handle assholes. This man was undoubtedly an asshole.

Arms flailing, Romeo's elbow hit the tray, sending it flying across the tent. "What the fuck is wrong with you?" he bellowed.

"Me?" she snarled, twisting her hand to the right. He howled and doubled over, a string of curses garbled together. Spittle covered his mouth. Mimicking his earlier posture, she bent toward him, closing the distance. "You do not touch people without their permission. Money doesn't give you a free pass. This," she flicked his silk tie, "is shit."

Panting, he spat, "You're a crazy bitch."

Lydia chuckled, releasing him, her hand cramping. The blood rushed in her ears like a runaway train. She shook from a mixture of anger and adrenaline. It had been a while since her last physical altercation, and she felt sick to her stomach. "At least I'm not a sexual predator, dick."

People formed around them, pushing her aside, going to help the man. Ras gripped her forearm and guided her out of the crowd. He put his arm over her shoulders, shielding her from curious onlookers.

"Shit, Lydia," he breathed, glancing behind them. "That was badass and stupid."

On the brink of tears, she nodded. What was she thinking? "I know."

"The prick deserved it."

She sniffled. "I egged him on. I knew better."

Closing in on the house, Ras pulled her tighter. "Fuck him. He can't go around grabbing women; it's fucking disgusting. I hope you crushed his nuts. I hope they popped out of the sack, so he can't breed stupid into the next generation." He rambled when he was nervous. "I wish I had my phone. You scared the shit out of him."

"They're going to fire me." Lydia saw Ms. Barra stomping across the lawn, her expressions old school fire and brimstone.

Mr. Barra's baritone voice was calm on the phone. Lydia cradled the cell to her ear, watching Ms. Barra pacing several yards away. The last half-an-hour was tense and humiliating.

"Are you sure you're alright, Lydia?" Mr. Barra asked for the third time. "You know I take these types of incidents seriously. My number one concern is your safety on the job."

She nodded and inhaled, realizing he couldn't see her. "Yes, sir. I'm okay, just a little shook up. Again, I'm really sorry. I overreacted. I should have walked away. It's not okay to assault a guest."

"No, it isn't," he agreed. "I spoke with several family members, and everyone agrees to overlook the altercation. Between us, I think they wanted to avoid a police report. Seems he's got a reputation for mishandling romantic relationships."

The news wasn't a surprise. And Mr. Barra had a curious network of friends across the state. Lydia bet he touched base with certain people before calling the Bardotte residence. "Do you want me to leave? I can have my sister pick me up."

"And give them the satisfaction, I'd rather not. If you want to leave, I understand, but if you're up to staying, then you have my blessing. No need making a bigger fuss about things. Stay under the radar, maybe behind the scenes. Sound alright to you?"

"You know I'm always here to work, Mr. Barra," she stated.

After she returned the phone to Ms. Barra, Lydia waited for her new assignment. In the distance, holding a serving tray, Ras alternated between thumbs-up and thumbs-down signs. She gave a thumbs-up, and he waved, pleased.

While they sorted out the debacle, the bride and groom arrived for the grand entrance to kick off the reception. The servers hurried to bring out the dinner courses. Lydia hated leaving them short-handed. Even one person made a tremendous difference in the timing of getting meals from the kitchen to the tables.

"Whatever you say, Teddy. Yes, I understand. I'm not an idiot. I'll talk to you tomorrow." Ms. Barra ended the call with an aggressive tap of her thumb. Taking the time to smooth out her jacket, she swallowed, blinking at Lydia. "You've caused nothing but problems today, Lydia."

"I'm sorry."

She held up her hand. "Apologies won't return that young man's dignity, will they? No." Fluffing her curly brown hair, permed and teased into an unpleasing coiffe, Ms. Barra derived pleasure from making Lydia uncomfortable. "I'm placing you behind the bar. You're assisting Ciel, do whatever she needs."

Head down, Lydia exhaled. She wanted to argue, wanted to remind Ms. Barra—well, it didn't matter. She still had her job and hadn't been sent home without pay. "I appreciate the second chance, Ms. Barra."

"Go on," she barked, waving her hand. "You're paid by the hour."

The strands of twinkling lights wrapped in the floral garland above the hand-painted bar sign sparkled off the various glassware. Behind the bar, Ciel cut lemons into thin, round slices. The rhythmic noise of the knife hitting the cutting board blended with the band's contemporary beat.

"Hey, Lydia," Ciel welcomed, glancing up from her project. "Need something?"

"I'm here to help." She wiped her damp hands on her thighs. "Ms. Barra sent me. I know I can't pour drinks, but I'll do whatever else you need."

Ciel set down the knife and layered the lemon slices into a glass bowl. "Does this have something to do with the commotion in the tent?"

Glossing over the details, Lydia summarized the altercation and the consequences. Older than most of the servers, Ciel was as a neutral party as possible. In her mid-forties, she doled out her motherly wisdom when asked, but kept her opinions to herself otherwise. She did her shift, kept a tidy workspace, and went home.

"Always some idiot, isn't there?" Ciel tossed an apron to Lydia and motioned to step through the entranceway. "I'd call the police on my boys if they acted that way. No crying for mamma then."

Lydia believed her. "Your boys are always polite. I don't think you have to worry."

"They're morons. But I forgive them; it's hard being a teenager." She slid over a bowl of washed limes and lemons, along with the knife and cutting board. "They'd like your pink hair. Both have a little crush on you. It's adorable."

The comfortable small chat was refreshing. With dinner service in progress, the only people at the bar were servers with the guests' requests. Wine and champagne didn't suit every palate.

After cutting the citrus fruit, Lydia took a sizeable gray plastic tote to collect abandoned glassware. Marketed as a "green" wedding, the hosts used as little plastic and paperware as possible. To keep up with the drinks for later in the evening, glassware needed to be washed.

Lydia pretended she was on a scavenger hunt. She awarded a point system to the different glass types. In minutes, she filled the tote and earned seventy-five points. She dropped it off in the kitchens, ready to load into the industrial dishwasher. Armed with another bin, she headed out for another round. It took four trips to fill the dishwasher, less than twenty minutes of wandering the property. One of the kitchen's staff, an older man with a stylish mustache, offered to run the machine when Lydia stared at the multi-button monster in utter confusion.

"It's a thirty-minute cycle," he replied as he punched a large button with his thumb. "They'll come out sparkling clean."

Lydia thanked him. "I'll set a timer. There'll be a lot of thirsty people needing these."

"I'll need a few before the night's finished," he joked, patting his thin belly.

On the quick trip back to the bar, Lydia watched the

sunset. The western horizon, blocked by treetops, and the stables in the distance, glowed a burnished copper with striations of pink and scarlet. Bilious clouds reflected the last rays as the sun dipped below the earth's curvature. It was beautiful out in the country. She never saw sunsets like this in her part of Lexington.

"Lydia, right?"

Hearing her name, she swiveled her head. The photographer, the nice one, waved to her. She waved back. He looked about as tired as she felt.

"I wanted to apologize for my colleague," he offered, stopping an arm's length from her. "For what she insinuated. It was rude and unlike her. She can come off as impolite, but it's her personality. She's just blunt sometimes. But what she said, that was rude."

Lydia waited, amused by his stumbling, apologetic explanation. She reached out and patted his arm with her fingertips when he finished. "It's alright, Aurelius. I forgot all about that, really. Weddings are stressful. People get rude."

Something in her tone caught his curiosity. "Rough night?" he queried, his dark eyebrows pressed together in displeasure.

Breathing from her diaphragm, Lydia nodded.

"Me too."

She noticed he rubbed the back of his neck again. An unconscious habit? It had boyish appeal, like a child caught doing something naughty but charming enough to get away with it. They stood together, not speaking.

Underneath the noise, the late summer insects hummed. A gentle breeze picked up, carrying a hint of coolness. Lydia needed to get out of the city. Maybe she and Miah could take a trip to Natural Bridge State Park before it got too cold.

Another round of clapping erupted from the tent, breaking her moment of contemplation. She patted down her tie, preparing to go back. Ciel needed the help, and she planned on being an exemplary employee the rest of the night.

"Do these look alright?" she asked him, checking the sprigs of foliage in her bun.

Inspecting her hair, he adjusted two pieces, securing them in place. "There we are," he said as he tilted his head. "Feel okay with you?"

"Better, thanks." She gave a quick grin. "Good luck out there."

He offered a grin. "Same to you."

Aurelius

PEOPLE SWARMED THE DANCE FLOOR. THE BAND played a decent cover of Cyndi Lauper's *Girls Just Wanna Have Fun*. Colorful flashing lights and the hefty sound system turned the tent into a concert venue. At some point, the musical acts changed. The new band wore vintage leather and ripped jeans, flannel shirts, beanies, a time capsule of the hipster movement. The male lead singer swayed his hips on the make-shift stage, grinding against the microphone stand. With the alcohol flowing from the bar, the suggestive motion garnered aggressive catcalls.

The migraine Aurelius refused to acknowledge settled in for the long haul. The blood vessels along the left side of his head pulsated with the upbeat music. He squeezed the bridge of his nose; the pressure winning out over the pain for a moment of relief. The contrast of the bright lights against the dark night zapped his pupils with each contraction, sending jolts into his brain. He longed for a pair of sunglasses.

During the meal, the speeches, and the obligatory first dances, Aurelius avoided further tête-à-têtes with the Kendricks. He was the person behind the camera, present but unseen.

Now he loomed in the periphery, watching the couple dance, considering the mechanics of the relationship. Monogamy wasn't for everyone. But why get married? An armchair philosopher, he wanted to ask the nitty-gritty questions. He suspected that broaching the topic would give the Kendricks false expectations he wanted to take part in their lifestyle. He wished the couple all the best in their endeavors, but he wanted nothing to do with their kink. Building his business was his number one priority. He lacked time to deal with his own issues. Adding a complex relationship—or any relationship—into the mix was not on his radar.

Pulling himself from his wandering thoughts, Aurelius inventoried the day's shots. They checked off all the essentials on the list. His SD card had several thousand photos, and he assumed Cyndi's had a similar number.

Close to nine o'clock, the wedding had turned to the celebration phase. By his reckoning, they were done for the night. He caught Cyndi with her camera to her eye, adjusting the aperture for the low light. Aurelius skirted the thin section between the tables and dance floor to reach her. He tapped her arm and motioned for her to follow him.

Halfway between the tent and the house, the music reached conversational level. Cyndi let her camera rest against her chest and stretched out her long arms. Although she put in nine hours, her makeup was smudge-free, and she kept impeccable posture. Aurelius's back burned from contorting and squatting all day.

"What's up?" Cyndi asked, rolling her neck.

She was great at compartmentalizing. On the outside, she appeared collected and calm. She bided her time, waiting to strike at him for the slight against her earlier judgment call. On the rare occasion, they had an argument, like every working relationship. People were people; it happened.

"Ready to wrap it up? I think we're finished." He brought up the app and scrolled through their checklist again. "I don't think we're missing anything."

Not bothering to open the app, she replied, "Whatever you say, boss."

Fine. If Cyndi wanted to delve into it, he'd play. His migraine lowered his tolerance for human interactions. "What's going on with you tonight?" He heard the terse undertone in his voice.

"With me?" She put a hand to her chest and bent forward. In her heels, her nose was inches from his. "I'm not the problem here."

He put up his hands in defense. "I'm at a loss. Everything seemed fine this morning. I can't fix anything if you don't tell me what's happened."

Eyes widening with fury, she poked him in the

shoulder with her finger, driving her acrylic nail into his muscle. "My work is second rate." *Poke.* "Its quality lacks the substance needed for solo gigs." *Poke.* "I should stick to shitty editorials and stock photos." *Poke.*

Stepping back, he shielded his shoulder from further assault. "What are you talking about? Who said that?"

"The damned articles," she cried out. "They're a testament to your ego. Aurelius Montanari: wedding photography's hip new style. You're a one-man show, running your business without any help at all. Oh wait, you've got a wanna-be groupie hanging on your coattails. Better cut her loose before she drags you down."

"Cyndi, I—"

"I'm a joke. Did you see the photos they ran? They chose abstract pieces from my college portfolio. Who the hell looks at those? I took those ten years ago. I was a kid!" She threw her hands up for emphasis, pacing in a small circle. "No one will hire me. Why did you do it? I don't get it. I really don't."

Offended by her accusation, Aurelius crossed his arms. He wanted to raise his voice, to shout back, to tell her she was an idiot. When had he ever acted against her best interest? If she was reasonable, she could see he had nothing to gain by the so-called betrayal. Since meeting her, he did everything to build up her career, not demolish it.

A piece of advice his mom gave him in high school surfaced: a person couldn't be emotional and reasonable at the same time. He didn't exactly understand it as a teenage boy, but his mom was a wise woman. Cyndi's emotions were through the stratosphere. No matter what he said, she'd take offense. Let the raging bull rage.

"I don't know what the articles say," he began, using an even tone, "but I assure you, I sabotaged nothing. My guess is they contacted your old professor for the portfolio. I sent in a selection from your upcoming gallery show. Call them. I had to get their permission since they agreed to host the event."

Her manic pace slowed. "The Red Note Collection?"

Nodding, Aurelius rubbed his throbbing arm. "I've told you, it's amazing."

Cyndi paused and covered her face with her palms. Her shoulders shook, and he realized she was laughing. The soft chuckle grew into a fit. Tears streamed down her cheeks, and she wiped them away with her hand.

"All day, I wanted to ream you out," she confessed between gasps for air. "I planned an entire speech and everything."

"And now?"

Rolling her eyes, she straightened her spine. "Now, I'm writing to those magazine's editors. Their staffing is atrocious, and I want them to write a correction." She leaned her arm against his and dabbed at her face. "I'm sorry, Aurelius. Everything got to me today. I'm usually better at it, you know, juggling all the needy people. There is something about this one, and it got under my skin."

He agreed. They couldn't cash the check fast enough and put it behind them.

Riding the positive vibes of mended fences, they went to pack up the equipment. Cyndi had designated a corner of the study as their operation base. It was out of the way and somewhat accessible. She kept everything in organized chaos, one of her many talents. They shared light, companionable banter as they sorted the gear and put it in the correct bags.

Cyndi's phone buzzed on the desk, startling them. "Must be Duke. I told him it'd be a late one." She put the DSLR case aside and picked up her phone. The screen's glow highlighted her sour expression. "It's Bianca. She wants to know if we can stay later. They're doing a big exit. Wardrobe change, fancy car. Gag me."

Aurelius let his head slump. "Sure, why not? I've got nothing better to do with my weekend."

"I'll stay. Let me stay. Think of it as an apology gift." Her thumbs hovered over the screen, ready to type a reply.

"Go home, have a late dinner with Duke, and we'll regroup on Monday," he said as he switched out batteries and SD cards. "One of us needs a life."

Lydia

CIEL MIXED DRINKS WHILE LYDIA CUT garnishes or served the bottled beer. After Ciel gave her a crash course in mixology, she fixed the mocktails and tonic waters. She avoided touching the alcohol bottles.

When hired on, Lydia made one request, to never work the bar. Ms. Barra's retribution was petty, but swift. Pouring drinks was Lydia's nightmare job. She had a substance abuse problem in high school. What started as sneaking sips of her mom's vodka on the weekends became a real addiction. She wasn't a violent drunk, but imbibing led to episodes of self-harm.

A late-night altercation with a cop had led to a minor drug charge. The small bag of weed changed everything. When she broke her probation, she had two choices: juvenile detention or enrollment into a state-run rehab program. Six months of daily counseling left her a different teenager.

Her phone buzzed again. Someone tried to call Lydia for the third time in the last five minutes. Lydia patted her pocket, wanting to sneak a peek in the lull. She couldn't afford a smartwatch or smartphone; hers was an old-fashioned flip phone. The line was five deep and growing. Her phone vibrated for the fourth time.

"Ciel, can I take a bathroom break?" She dumped crushed iced into waiting glasses.

Ciel flipped the cocktail shaker over her hand and then opened the lid and poured out the martini. The little show garnered applause from the tipsy woman and her friend. She shoved money into the overflowing tip jar.

"Yeah, I've got this." She plopped a green olive into the glass and handed it to the woman. "You need a break, anyway. It's been hours."

Untying her wet apron, Lydia set it on an empty stool. "I'll try to hurry. Don't want to leave you alone for too long."

"Don't rush, alright. Take your full break. Grab something to eat, stretch your legs. I'll be okay here," Ciel said, channeling her innate maternal concern. "Bring me back a sandwich or something. I'm starved."

"Will do!" Her voice trailed as she scampered from the bar. Confident she was out of sight, Lydia dug her phone from her pocket and flipped open the top. Miah's number. Cold fear crept from her toes to her thighs. She held in number two on the keypad for a quick redial.

"Lydia!" Miah answered. She sounded breathy, panicked.

"What's wrong?" Lydia cupped the phone to block out the outside noise. She jogged further out onto the lawn. "Can you hear me?"

"I'm sorry. I shouldn't have called while you were at work." Her words slurred as her violent crying overtook her.

Mind racing to the worst possible scenarios, Lydia felt her heart palpitate. "Is it your blood sugar? What are your readings? Miah, talk to me. Are you okay? Call an ambulance. Don't drive."

Through the thick sniffles, Miah managed somewhat complete sentences. It was her mom, Angel. She was in jail. Miah had been her one phone call.

"But she's okay, right?" Lydia asked. "Not hurt or anything?"

"No. I don't know," Miah wept. "She's not hurt. I think drugs are involved. She said she needed a lawyer, but I don't have any money. Where am I going to get a lawyer?"

She wanted to say it wasn't Miah's problem. Angel got herself into the situation. She was a big girl; she knew the potential consequences of dating a pill-popper. Tough love would come. Now it would only hurt Miah's feelings. She needed her sister's support.

Stress triggered a response. Lydia's gut reaction was to leave, drive to the jail, and ream out Angel. Instead, she pinched her thigh to the point it would bruise. "If it comes to that, the court will assign someone. That's what happened to me, remember? Jail is scary, and she's freaking out. That's normal, right? Who wouldn't freak out? Do you need me to come home?"

Miah's breathing evened, the initial shock wearing away. "No, no, you're right. I panicked, but everything will be fine." She gave a weak laugh, trying to lighten her reaction. "You're always so calm in these situations, and I'm a mess."

"It's okay to be a mess. She's your mom," Lydia said. "I can come home if you need me. This is important."

"Really, it's okay. I'm headed to her house to check the cats. I'll see you when you get home. Be careful, it's late. I'll see you soon." The phone went dead.

Beneath the twinkling fairy lights of an outbuilding, Lydia put her hands on her knees and groaned. Dread cramped her middle like a searing hot vice. She carried her stress in her stomach and felt the gurgle of indigestion bubbling up in her throat.

A darkened figure stepped around the building. "Do you need help?"

Surprised, heart flying into her throat, Lydia yelped. She jumped upright and stumbled, almost toppling to the ground. Regaining her balance, she cried, "Don't do that!"

"I didn't mean to eavesdrop." He moved under the lights, hands up in surrender. "Lydia?"

Squinting against the night, her skin prickled. She

gave an uneasy chuckle as the tension dissipated in her chest. "It's like you're reverse stalking me."

Aurelius gave one barking laugh. "Just what a guy likes to hear, that he's a stalker."

"Sorry," she mumbled. "I'm not at my best."

"Why don't you sit for a minute? I've got some water and stole a plate from the kitchen." He held out his hand as an offering.

Food would help settle her stomach. She followed him around to the building's front. Just inside, she saw an overturned crate with his pilfered snacks. Lydia shoved a cold tomato-feta bite into her mouth and chewed. It tasted amazing.

"Why are you out here?" she asked with a full mouth.

Reaching to the floor, he retrieved a bottle of water. "Migraine. I can't stand the music and lights. They make me nauseous." He put the bottle between them.

Lydia undid the lid and poured the lukewarm water into her mouth. She half-missed, and some dribbled down her chin. It was better than getting floaters in his drink. Disregarding manners, she used her sleeve to wipe at her face. "Sorry, I've heard those are bad."

"It's one of those things. Could be worse," Aurelius said and chose one of the elitist grilled cheese triangles.

Close up, he looked haggard, like he could use a good night's sleep, a long shower, and a hot coffee. Lydia reconsidered. Maybe she needed those things and was projecting. Either way, the night couldn't end soon enough.

Swiping her hands together to remove the crumbs, Lydia guessed her break was over. Her grumbling stomach reminded her to grab something for Ciel. Midnight was a long way off.

"Thanks for this." Lydia wanted to linger. All day they had half-conversations, interrupted by providence. "Seems we're always going in opposite directions." She went to the doorway and hesitated. "Oh, and I don't think you're a stalker. My brain's distracted, and some-times my filter disappears."

He blinked and squinted his left eye. "I'll remember that for next time."

As she stepped up, her shoelace snagged the corner of the door. As she bent to release the lace, her shoulder bumped the door, closing it. "Can you be a bigger klutz?" she muttered to herself. Lydia tried the handle.

Locked.

Aurelius

"Ah, we have a problem." Lydia jerked on the pull handle. The door shook with her effort but remained closed.

Light came in from the barred windows set high in the building's wall. Turning on his phone's light, Aurelius pointed it at the closing mechanism. It looked old, maybe the original hardware. "I don't see a lock." He tried. It wouldn't budge.

She bent to examine the handle too. Her fingers traced the metalwork, searching for a release or button, he suspected. A small gap formed between and door and the frame. For a modern doorknob to catch and lock, the latch went into a recessed groove in the frame. He saw no internal latch.

Heavy-limbed, Lydia moved aside. "I bet it's on the outside. A slide lock or something. These old places have its own personality."

He checked his phone. No signal. So much for the best coverage in the country! For what he paid a month, he should have service in a coal mine three miles deep.

"I can't call out either." Lydia examined an ancient flip phone.

Aurelius braced his foot against the stone wall and pulled. Nothing. He tried again, straining the muscles in his arms and back. The exertion increased the pounding in his head, forcing him to stop. "Were they expecting a zombie invasion? This is solid."

"Not zombies."

"Oh right," he replied, and almost laughed at himself. "I give it to 1800s craftmanship. The damn Yankees weren't getting in here. Not so good for us, though."

Going to the hinges, she asked for his phone. "To be fair, they considered Kentucky a border state for a reason. They weren't all Confederates." Lydia tested the pin between the two ornate metal wings. "If we had a hammer and a screwdriver, maybe we could get out the middle pieces. But then, the door might crush us before we got out of the way."

"That's something."

"The Confederates or the door?" She returned the phone and wiped her hands on her pants, leaving dusty palm prints on the black fabric.

"All of it, I guess." Aurelius scanned the narrow rectangular windows. Regardless of the bars, he couldn't fit through them. Lydia was short, maybe five foot two. But again, the bars were in the way.

Distracted, he heard the distinct sound of water. Closing the door amplified the noises inside. "Do you hear running water? It's not raining out. I can still see the stars."

"Shine your light towards the back," she instructed.

They navigated past the toppled crates and boxes. The sound grew, like a running creek or water in a street gutter after a storm. The light reflected off a square in the stone floor, cut away to reveal clear rippling water.

Lydia bent and dipped her fingers in the water. "This is a springhouse."

"A what?"

"Do you ever get out of the city?" she asked as she flicked water at him.

He wiped the droplets from his pant legs. "Not if I can help it. Look what happens when I do?"

"Fair enough." She rolled up her sleeves to her elbows, revealing colorful tattoos on both arms. Crouching, she dipped in her hands and brought it to her face. He went to warn her not to drink it, but stopped. She splashed down her cheeks and forehead. "It's refreshing if you want to try. The water's clean; it's a spring. Probably a deep aquifer feeding different ones all over this area. The original owners built this to protect it from contamination. Springs are valuable resources."

Good to know they had emergency water if needed. Aurelius bent and touched the water. It was icy cold. He pulled the useless decorative handkerchief from his breast pocket, dunked it in, and squeezed out the excess water. Wonderful relief! He pressed the cold compress against his temple.

"That's nice," he sighed, aware he looked like a fashionable pirate. "How do you know all this stuff?"

"When I was a kid, my mom dated this real history nerd. A good guy, really smart. He brought us to all these battlefields and museums. We went to a few of his war reenactments." Lydia patted her face again. "I guess it stuck. History's interesting, but I really liked just being around him. There weren't many good ones, so if he wanted to spend a Saturday reliving a battle or whatever, I didn't complain."

He couldn't relate. If the Montanaris weren't at the family restaurant, they stayed at home, finding ways to assimilate by hosting themed parties, pushing him into sports, forcing him to play with the neighbor kids. A typical middle-class childhood, as he saw it.

"Is your mom okay?" He thought of an explanation when she gave him an odd look. "I overheard you earlier. I wasn't trying to pry."

"Ah, yeah," she replied, nodding. "It's my sister's mom. She's in jail." She stood and shook out her legs. "Why don't you sit? It's a long story."

Settled on a crate, the cool handkerchief covering half his face, he watched her. Lydia walked in a slow circle, avoiding the detritus. To stop his neck from getting a crick, he kept his focus straight ahead. This meant she bobbed in and out of his line of vision.

"So, my sister and I, we have the same dad. I guess we're technically half-sisters, but we grew up in each other's houses, so it never felt that way. Her mom and my mom used to work together and became good friends. They shared a lot of things, and I guess at some point, they shared our dad." She looked as if she swallowed pickle brine. "Gross, I know. Anyway, Miah's mom got arrested. She's been with this drug-head, and well, you make your bed, you know."

Aurelius imagined a corkboard with red string signifying people and their relationships like the cops on TV. There were a few knots in there for sure, and loop-de-loops, hell maybe some braids. Regardless of missing at least a third of her explanation, he enjoyed hearing her talk. She had a soothing voice, one fit for all those meditation apps or audiobooks.

"I'll have to find the money or something. I don't know. It's not a great time. Well, is it ever a great time to get arrested?" Lydia plopped down across from him, huffing. "See, it's good and bad, the family situation."

"The bride asked me to be in a threesome with her husband," he blurted. Telling someone else, releasing that statement into the universe, made him feel lighter. Why, at this point, he guessed it was a mixture of the minor anxiety of never being found and full-blown exhaustion.

Her mouth popped open. "And?"

"And it was bizarre."

She motioned with her hands for him to go on and leaned forward. "She's intimidating."

"Right? Like, I'm going to get the leather and whips, put on a giant strap on, and you're at my mercy, intimidating."

Snorting, Lydia waved her hand in front of her. "Oh my. I didn't need that picture in my head."

"It's in my head, and I'm giving it to you," he countered, grinning. "It was flattering. Who doesn't like a nudge to their ego every once in a while?"

She tapped her finger against her chin. "Yeah, she is hot. Definitely the better looking of the two. Not that he's terrible, he's a solid eight. You could do worse." Her eyes went blank. "I've so many questions, like how does it work? Is there a safe word or words? Who goes where?"

"We'll never know." He tossed the wet handkerchief at her, and she jumped. "Do you think they'll find us?"

"Eventually. I can try shouting out a window." Lydia raised her gaze upwards. "Maybe someone will hear me."

It was worth a try. Together, they built a precarious platform from junk. Aurelius figured a group of ten-year-olds could do a better job. Lydia climbed up, her mouth reaching the window's lip.

"If you want to cover your ears, I don't mind," she noted, her hands gripping two bars for stability. "This is going to get annoying, fast."

Lydia

Lydia was tired of hearing her voice. For her amusement, she tried different accents. Her attempt at Australian was atrocious. French, not too bad. Russian turned out to be a mix of the American South with a dash of Golem from *Lord of the Rings*.

Her arm ached. She held it against the rough stone, waving it back and forth like an idiot. Between her calls, she stopped and listened for a reply. The band continued its litany of cover songs, which was helpful.

Aurelius sat on the ground, his head propped against the wall, ears covered by his hands. He looked miserable. If she had another option, she would try. Aside from her horrendous cries for help, she was at a loss.

She considered burning the door down and then nixed it right away. They'd likely die of smoke inhalation. How would she start a fire, anyway? No way she could remove the bars, either. With a stone floor and no tools, digging under the walls was out. The spring house had solid construction.

If I were a fish, I could swim out.

Rubbing her dry eyes, she ignored the crazy, random thought. She rolled her burning shoulders and switched arms. Her right hand hit the slight bulge in her pocket. Her cell phone.

Taking care, Lydia held it up to the window. No bars. She stretched out the window; the phone held at the end of her reach.

One tiny signal bar showed on the screen.

"Aurelius," she said, too afraid to move. When he didn't answer, she repeated his name with force.

"Huh? What?" Using the wall, he got to his feet. "Is someone there?"

"I've got one bar of signal. But my arm's not long enough to hit the buttons."

Removing his suit jacket, he tossed it aside. He tested each step of their platform before committing his total weight. It was smart, but it annoyed her anyway. Her arm muscles seared, and she needed to pee.

Widening his stance, he stood behind her. Aurelius inched his arm out the window and cradled the hand and phone in his open hand. "I've got it," he whispered against the crown of her head.

"Are you sure?"

"I swear. You can drop it."

They stared as her trembling fingertips released the phone. It landed in his palm.

She inhaled. "Thank you, Jesus."

Maneuvering out of his way, she twisted and turned like an amateur contortionist. She apologized for bumping or brushing against him. The close-quarters made it impossible not to touch. Still, she needed to verbalize the awkwardness.

Trapped inside a building was awful, but at least she wasn't alone. As a stranger, Aurelius was a decent survival partner. Better than most of her friends, if she had to guess.

He was in position to dial a number. "Who do we call?"

"Your assistant, Cyndi. She's here, right?" Lydia suggested.

"I sent her home." Aurelius concentrated. "In my phone is the bride's number. Or how about the police?"

Already going for his phone, she leapt to the floor and dashed to grab the device. He gave her the key code to unlock it. She read the number to him. His thumb pressed each digit with precision, and then he hit the green call button.

Ring.

Ring.

Ring.

"Hello, you've reached Bianca Bardotte. I'm unable to answer the phone. Please leave your name, number, and a brief message, and I will return your call." *Beep. Beep. Beep.*

Angry, he hit redial. Three times. Bianca didn't answer her cell phone.

"Any other suggestions?" he asked.

Lydia climbed back up, relying on the wall for support. "Hold in number four. It's my friend Ras. He's another server tonight. We're not supposed to have our phones on, but we may get lucky." She prayed he had his phone. He almost always kept it in his pocket.

Two rings. Ras answered, "Lydia, where are you? The Leech has moved beyond pissed to *pisst*."

"Ras!" Lydia shoved her face to the bars. "We need help."

"Honey, you need all sorts of help. Like call down the angels, maybe a few saints, I don't know, Jesus couldn't hurt."

"Shut up, will you! We need help. We're stuck. The door locked, and we can't get out," she shouted. She felt her head bumping Aurelius's elbow. He adjusted his grip.

A loud, creaking crack filled her ears. The floor disappeared beneath them.

* * *

AURELIUS

DUST AND DIRT COATED HIS MOUTH. AURELIUS lay on his back. Something heavy draped around his midsection pinned him down. He heard a low, long groan and felt the thing shift. Lydia sat up, and he inhaled a deep breath.

"Are you okay?" she coughed.

A fine layer of pale dust covered her whole body. Her hair hung like a mangled octopus around her head. She pawed at her face, smearing dirt in streaks.

Besides overall body pain, he felt like he survived unscathed. "Nothing's broke. You?"

"I tweaked my ankle. It'll be fine, I think. Feels like I twisted it or something. I'm not worried." She scanned the remnants of their scaffolding. "The phone!" Hoping up, she hobbled, favoring her right leg, and used her hands to push aside broken bits and pieces.

Rising, Aurelius kicked at the floor. He struggled to see through the floating dust. Several minutes into the search, Lydia moaned and held up her busted phone. During the avalanche, something broke it at the hinge, ripping it in two.

"Will this day never end?" She looked skyward and tossed the broken pieces to the floor.

He coaxed her to sit and drink from the water bottle. A large tear in her shirt cut across her back. She bent forward, and he checked for scrapes or punctures. She got away clean, not even a red mark.

"That's something." She gave him the bottle. "Maybe it was enough. There can't be too many buildings."

"Right. They'll find us." He made his tone light and cheery.

Lydia suggested they wash up in the spring. Feeling

the grit between his teeth, he agreed. They hovered over the square hole, dousing cold water on exposed skin. Aurelius tested the depth, then dunked his entire head in, glad he had short hair. He came up gasping for air, wide-eyed and smiling. "That's better than any espresso I've ever had."

"I'll take your word." She undid her hair, fluffed it with her fingers, and wound it on top of her head. The pink strands stuck out in every direction like an indecisive porcupine.

"I saw you earlier," he stated.

Frowning, she reached out and touched his forehead. "Are you sure you're okay? Did you hit your head?"

"No, I mean, I remember the hair. The pink. When I arrived, you and some woman, there was an argument. For what it's worth, I think it suits you."

She touched her hair, rubbing an end through her fingers. "Thanks. It was spontaneous."

The compliment conjured tears, not his intention. Lydia sniffled and lifted her head, trying to force them back. Useless, he held out his hand to her, and she accepted, squeezing his palm. She wavered for a minute, controlled her emotions, and nodded as if prepared to face down the worst-case scenario: post-apocalypse zombies, a pool of flesh-eating piranhas, an impenetrable locked door.

Giving her a moment, Aurelius went to the front of the building. He put together two small crates and pushed them against the wall. For padding, he wadded up dry-rotted burlap bags and tied them with rope. The best sleeping accommodations in Chez Spring House.

Lydia reappeared, her arms hugging her chest. "That looks cozy," she joked, toeing one of the burlap pillows.

"I want to think your mom's historian boyfriend would be proud." He picked up his suit jacket, flicked it to remove the dust, and held it up for her. "You're cold, and it's getting colder. Take it."

She inserted one arm and chuckled when he helped her into the jacket. "That's a first."

"I'm here all night, ladies and gentleman."

Not long or wide enough for him, Aurelius gave her the crates to sleep on. She protested, but he countered she needed to elevate her ankle. With no response to his illogical argument, Lydia acquiesced. He tucked a burlap roll under her left calf and covered her the best he could.

He lay on the floor and used one partial burlap bag as a barrier against the cold stone. Sleep was impossible, but he propped his head on his arm and rolled on his side, eyes fixed on the door.

"His name was Denver."

"Whose name?" he questioned her.

She answered, her voice small and quiet. "The historian's. His name was Denver. He hated the Denver Broncos."

Aurelius

THE COMPUTER SCREEN SHOWED IMAGES OF smiling boys in their football uniforms. Aurelius opened the main folder and scanned the sub-folders labeled with surnames. The last of the e-mails went out to the parents, a link with a specific code to download the photo pack along with a release form to duplicate as they see fit.

He reached for his coffee and sipped. Ice cold. No matter, he downed it anyway and padded to the sink in his socks. The single plate he used last night waited to be washed. He added the dirty coffee cup.

Upstairs, he showered to wash away the shame of wearing the same pajamas for three days. He put on comfortable jeans, a local band t-shirt, and a blue hoodie. His phone rang, and he checked the caller. Unknown. He hit ignore. Two weeks out, he thought the incident at the Bardotte-Kendrick wedding would be old news. The reporters called his personal cell, his work phone, they emailed, they contacted his parents and Cyndi for statements. They were the epitome of relentless. It was disgraceful and borderline stalking.

A glimmer of normality surfaced when Jordan invited him to the UK football game. Aurelius needed out of his house and headspace. A meeting of teams on the gridiron, beer and nachos, chatting with an old friend, that was good medicine.

With an hour to go, he parked his jeep outside Jordon's apartment. Aurelius scrolled through his e-mail, deleting everything suspicious. Reporters were worse than spammers.

The innocent situation got flipped on its head. When he tried to clarify, he exacerbated the problem. By not speaking, it fed speculation, but at least they couldn't twist his words to fit their agenda.

No one wanted the truth.

They wanted to push a scintillating version where Lydia coerced him into the outbuilding and held him hostage. Various reasons floated around on her motivations: money, delusional breakdown, obsession.

Kentucky's elite relied on limited services for their events. Unbeknownst to both parties, he and Lydia were at the same wedding last year. A Ms. Barra of Barra Hospitality confirmed the date and time on a local morning program, and the segment looped on for several days. This unremarkable circumstance fueled conspiracies, which Lydia's ex-supervisor offered several of her own.

The woman painted a contradictory portrait of Lydia as an unreliable, spastic, and violent employee. Several people rose to her defense, a local church's pastor a notable character reference, but the damage hit its mark. Lydia Hest's reputation lay in tatters, and Aurelius Montanari came out the victim of an imagined crime.

What happened was neither newsworthy nor tantalizing. Around sunrise, Lydia woke to the sound of groundskeepers cleaning. She cried out, scaring the shit out of Aurelius, as he'd been half-asleep, shivering, dreaming about swimming in a pool of ice cubes.

The men had opened the door, releasing them from their imprisonment. The outside metal latch was a known hazard on the property. In the dark, Aurelius and Lydia missed the posted warning sign of the danger.

To his surprise, Mr. Bardotte had offered copious apologies. He'd brought them to the house's informal kitchen, percolated fresh ground coffee, and served them European-style breakfast pastries. Without his wife hovering, he was a congenial host.

Mr. Bardotte and Aurelius had volunteered to drive Lydia home, but she'd declined, calling her sister for a ride. Her ankle had continued to ache and showed minor swelling. She'd decided, after much debate, to get it checked. Having connections throughout the city, Mr. Bardotte had phoned a physician associated with the university's hospital. He'd agreed to see Lydia on Mr. Bardotte's dime.

The last time Aurelius saw her, Lydia was in her

sister's car. She'd leaned out the window, thanking Mr. Bardotte for his generosity. She acted like a normal person during the entirety of their interactions. The pastor's description seemed spot on—personable, kind, hard-working, unique, somewhat awkward, but in an endearing way.

"Hey man, ready for the game?" Jordon asked as he opened the jeep's passenger door.

Shoving his phone in the cup holder, Aurelius mumbled, "Let's go, Wildcats."

"It's not possible for you to speak with her." The intimidating woman glowered behind the counter. Dressed in black overalls and a black shirt, she gripped her pencil in two hands. "If it concerns tattoo work, you can leave a message with me."

Aurelius spent a week trying to locate Lydia. The search included close to a dozen phone calls and hours scouring the internet. By dumb luck, he stumbled upon one random blog post mentioning a Lydia as an up-and-coming tattooist near Lexington. Following a tangled hop from site to site, one he was confident he couldn't recreate, he ended at the website for The Illustrated Woman Tattoo Parlour.

"I understand why you're hesitant. With everything that happened, I'm the same way." He fished out a business card from his jacket's inner pocket. "I'm not a journalist or whatever."

Suspicious, she plucked the card from his hand and examined it. "Ah, so you're the asshole," she stated and flicked the card across the room. "Sorry, never heard of what's-er-name. If that's all you needed, looks like you got your answer."

"Please, can I leave her a message at least? I'm not an asshole, really. The whole thing—"

"Listen, Mr. Montanari, I don't care." She let the pencil drop to her desk and put her hands on her slim hips. "It's not my business. You should take it elsewhere."

He recognized defeat. Aside from outright stalking Lydia, this was his last chance of contacting her. Stoop-shouldered, he turned and headed for the exit. Not everything could be fixed. Cyndi warned him to leave it alone.

Closing in on the door, he heard a familiar voice. With its soft intonations, the feminine lilt caused his abdomen to tighten. A flash of unexpected anticipation spread through his limbs. "Lydia?" he questioned.

Coming down a long hall, she faltered mid-step, a stack of manilla files in her hand. Her blond and pink hair hung in loose curls. Wearing a tank top, her colorful tattoo sleeves stretched from wrist to her shoulders. Through all the hubbub, Aurelius forgot how attractive he found her. Lydia was a breath of quirky fresh air against the styled replicants he saw day in and out.

"Hey," she answered and entered the seating area. "What are you doing here?"

"Looking for you, actually." He waited, unsure what to say. During the drive across the city, he ran through numerous scenarios. Now his mind was as blank as freshly fallen snow. "Is there somewhere we can talk?"

She tapped the folder and then glanced at the other woman. "Is it okay, Di? It won't take long."

Stuck in the same position, the woman shot bullets of dislike at Aurelius. "I'll be here if you need me."

"This way," Lydia offered with a wag of her hand. "I'm cleaning out a back storage room. We can talk there." Down the hall, past three occupied rooms, she let him enter the half-empty space first. The incandescent bulbs cast a harsh white light on the organized clutter. Lydia pointed at a padded office chair, and Aurelius sat.

Across from him, she leaned against a refurbished antique desk. "What do you need, Aurelius?" She crossed and uncrossed her ankles, flashing a pair of beat-up pink Chuck Taylors.

"I don't need anything," he replied in earnest. "Are you alright? All that happened. I don't know what to call it."

"Humiliating. Heart-breaking. Horrendous." She puffed out her cheeks and let out the air. "I'll be fine. We did nothing wrong, and everyone who matters knows the truth, so I guess that's what's important. How are you? Some of those interviews were uncomfortable to watch."

If he had to rate the experiences by excruciation level, this moment beat out all the interviews by miles. "It was like in the cartoons when the snowball rolls down a hill and grows until it crushes the town. No one listened to reason."

Nodding, she commiserated. "But how are you? The past month, not gotten much sleep, have you?" Lydia patted under her eyes. "Bags. I could pack my whole apartment in them."

He opened and closed his mouth like a floundering goldfish. "You know I'm vain, right?"

Smirking, she shook her head. "Wipe away my foundation and concealer, and I've got a matching set of luggage underneath. If it wasn't the phone calls, people followed me, or I imagined they followed me. I stayed a week at my friend's house until his boyfriend got weirded out by my paranoia and asked me to leave."

Aurelius gulped in air. He knew it would be bad, but not that bad. "I'm sorry. I don't know what else to say. It's pathetic. There should be a word or something that means more, you know."

"Having a bout of survivor's guilt?" She raised her brows at his confusion. "It's not the same term, I'm sure, but a similar principle. Or so my counselor says. She's smarter than me, so I'll leave it up to her.

"Anyway, don't feel guilty or sorry. What did you do? What did either of us do? I've accepted it, and that's all I can do. It was never in our control. I appreciate that you tried, though. That was brave, facing those people in my defense. When you didn't call back, I thought you wanted to put distance between us, so I didn't press it."

"When did you call?" Aurelius stood, the chair

pushed back by momentum. Had he deleted her messages by mistake? In all the confusion, it was more than possible.

Staring off, Lydia counted on her fingers. "A week or so later. Miah saw a replay of your interview. We looked up your business number and reached your assistant. I left several messages with her, but I stopped trying when I heard nothing. I didn't want to be a nuisance."

"Cyndi Postman, you're sure?"

"Hard to forget her," she countered. "She had the gallery show, right? Opened last weekend or something. Di went. Her wife is big on that type of art. They brought a flyer in, and I recognized her photo."

Chewing on the snippet of information, he wondered why Cyndi screened his phone calls. He planned on asking her as soon as he left. The notion felt like a betrayal. He hoped it was a misunderstanding, but he doubted it.

Lydia scribbled on an old piece of paper and tore off the corner. "Here, if you need to talk. Feel free to text or whatever. Besides here, I'm at home or church."

"You upgraded?" He pocketed her phone number.

"Flip phones are cool."

Amused, he replied, "Maybe twenty years ago."

"I'll walk you out," Lydia chuckled, "or I don't know what Di will do. She's been a little protective."

In the lobby, she gave him a quick hug and wished him the best. Aurelius caught a whiff of Lydia's perfume, a mix of something sweet and summery, like cotton candy, lemons, and strawberries. It summoned memories of mid-summer carnivals as a kid, with bright lights, laughter, and rickety rides.

Di stared at the interaction, distrusting his every movement. No chance of winning her over soon. Aurelius avoided eye contact as he said goodbye.

Under a cloudy October sky, he crossed to his jeep. Secure in his seat, he dug out his phone and hit Cyndi's number.

She answered on the fourth ring. "Need something, boss?"

"Explain why you decided not to tell me Lydia Hest called."

Lydia

In bed, the television showing a documentary on meerkats, Lydia used a stretchy band to flex the stiff tendon in her ankle. After hauling out the contents of the storage room, her healing sprain was swollen and stiff. She did her at-home therapy as instructed and saw incremental improvement. The amiable orthopedic physician had scheduled a follow-up visit as a preventative measure during the initial exam. The minor sprain didn't require the attention, and she hated wasting the man's time. When she called to cancel, the secretary put him on the phone, and she agreed to keep the appointment.

Finished with the exercises, Lydia put the band in her tiny closet and slipped into a well-worn cartoon pajama set. She grabbed her pad from her thrifted side table and made a note to contact Mr. Bardotte. From the onset of the fiasco, he was a surprising ally. To call him a friend would go too far, but he reined in the Bardotte-Kendrick contribution. He pressed on his nephew's previous indiscretions to keep the family in line. When the mania reached a fever pitch, she reached out to him in desperation. Within twenty-four hours, the media coverage almost shut down. Though he denied any involvement, Lydia suspected he touted his pull in the community.

Miah's voice filtered through the apartment's thin walls. For privacy, Lydia adjusted the TV's volume to prevent eavesdropping. Angel called like clockwork at Miah's expense, as she awaited her court hearing. Lydia tried to support her sister and stay oblivious to the case's details. So far, it was a losing battle.

Her phone rattled on the metal tabletop. She picked it up and glanced at the touch screen. A new text message from an unknown number.

UNKNOWN: HI LYDIA. THANK YOU FOR THIS afternoon. Again, I'm sorry for all the problems I inadvertently caused you and yours. Aurelius.

OUT OF COURTESY, SHE TYPED A QUICK REPLY and hit send. Seeing Aurelius was unexpected. When her attempts to reach him went unanswered, she speculated with Miah and Ras. They deduced his lack of response was to uphold his professional reputation. To hear he was unaware summoned a mixture of emotions.

Less than a minute later, a new message came through. Laying back on her pillows, Lydia undertook the chat with care. Texts passed back and forth, casual banter, like chatting with an acquaintance on the bus.

An hour turned into two, and then it was past midnight.

Miah went to bed. Her company had her training for six weeks. Then she would go solo in the coveted full-time position. To prepare, she stayed up late studying manuals. On a usual night, Lydia kept to her sister's routine. She switched off her lights and closed her door. Sneaking to her bed, the entire act reminded her of breaking curfew a decade ago, and she giggled in the dark.

Aurelius added innocent emojis, which grew somewhat flirty as the night progressed. If he'd thrown out the eggplant, banana, or tongue, anything resembling sexting, he would have won a blocked number.

Turned out, Aurelius was a big *Star Wars* geek. They passed Darth Vader and Storm Trooper memes back and forth. Then they debated between The Ramones or The Clash. Lydia liked both but played devil's advocate when discussing music. Somehow that segued into favorite breakfast foods.

By four a.m., Lydia fought to keep her eyelids open. Curled on her side, head under the blanket, she yawned and rubbed her eyes until she saw white spots dancing in her vision. If she didn't go to bed soon, she would need a constant coffee IV at the parlor later.

. . .

AURELIUS: ARE YOU HUNGRY?

Lydia:...

Lydia: It's four. I need my beauty sleep.

Aurelius: Wrong answer. Pancakes or waffles?

Lydia: Something with blueberries and cheese.

Aurelius: Together?

Lydia: Not my usual. I'd try it, I guess.

Aurelius: I'll pick you up. What's your address?

Lydia: I'm joking! I need sleep, crazy man.

Aurelius: If you don't tell me your address, I'll show up at your work. Which is worse? Tick Tock...Lydia. Tick Tock...

Epilogue

THE GROUP SPORTED PINK T-SHIRTS, A BRIGHT cluster in the crowded convention center. Ras leaned close to Aurelius as a bulky man pushed through on his way to the front. Aurelius saw the warning signs of Ras's temper and elbowed him in the side. "Not worth it."

"He's right," Di added, tugging at her shirt collar for the hundredth time. "Besides, he's a judge. Don't want to piss him off."

Lacking boundaries, Ras put a hand on Aurelius's shoulder and stood on tip-toe. "Where is she? It's been forever already."

The Lex-Tat convention's three-day event drew in tattoo enthusiasts from across the globe. The Illustrated Woman Tattoo Parlour's booth kept a steady stream of clients in their one chair. Artists took shifts, their appointments booked months in advance via the convention's online form. Ras manned the merchandise and hawked future bookings to locals.

Aurelius signed on as one of the convention's official photographers. His red badge gave him access to all events, and he took advantage of all the special panels. This tattoo community had an impressive, diverse culture. Artists specialized in specific styles drew onlookers, and most carried on amusing conversations as they transformed blank skin into a living masterpiece.

The air smelled of antiseptic spray and ink.

He snuck Lydia into a session hosted by a traditional Scandinavian tattooist. The soft-spoken woman had a commanding presence on stage. Her graying blond hair in long dreadlocks, wearing a handmade dress featuring vegetable dyes, she spoke of the importance of teaching historical techniques. Her faded blue sigils, the ink naturally sourced, aged with a grace not seen with modern technology.

A woman in a skin-tight red leather dress, high heels, and a magenta mohawk came on stage. The crowd quieted and leaned forward, waiting for her to speak.

Given a signal off-stage, she raised the mic to her painted black lips. "Good afternoon, everyone! Welcome back to the main stage. Thank you for your patience. This year, the novice competition took considerable time to judge with our ten talented contestants." She smiled, showing off dazzling white teeth. "Each tattooist brought in a healed example of their work. And we want to thank these men and women for letting our judges poke and prod. A big round of applause."

Ten people lined up on the stage. When Rat appeared, his wife, Tammy, shouted his name. Di and Marian patted her on the arm and offered encouraging words. The applause grew as the tattooists followed behind. Lydia stopped beside Rat and took his hand for comfort. She scanned the crowd, and when she spotted them, their pink shirts like beacons, Aurelius noticed the physical relief in her expression. She waved, and a dozen hands shot into the surrounding air.

To his right, Miah clutched his upper arm. "Oh, I'm so nervous for her."

"She'll be alright, either way," he said.

Squinting at him, a look he recognized too well, she replied, "She's going to win. I'm just nervous if she has to do a speech or something. Lydia is a terrible public speaker."

"And we have our talented tattooists," the woman continued. "Welcome them to the stage as they stand by their victims—I mean clients." A ripple of laughter. "Now, owner of Carnage Ink, Bario Soto will announce the judges' decisions."

The man who'd pushed past them earlier crossed the stage and accepted the microphone. "Hello everyone! As the lovely Ms. Garcia mentioned, this was a tough competition to judge. Ten talented newcomers to the tattoo community. Each has a budding style. I know we'll see them transform the industry. Shall we get to it?"

He called three names. Second runner-up, runner-up, and first place. At no point did he say Lydia Hest. The three tattooists accepted their certificates and monetary prizes. Doing his job, Aurelius maneuvered to the side and snapped photos of the winners.

It was bittersweet, seeing Lydia on stage, clapping. She smiled, happy for the winners. He had no doubt it was genuine.

"Okay, we're not done yet, ladies and gentleman," Bario announced and put his finger to his lips. When the clapping abated, he waited a moment in the dramatic quiet. Then he said, "Because we had such high-caliber entries in this division, the judges decided to award a special recognition based on composition, technical difficulty, and overall appearance. On behalf of Lex-Tat, I want to present Lydia Hest of The Illustrated Woman Tattoo Parlour with the Judge's Choice Award."

As Aurelius watched Lydia and Rat accept their certificates, he alternated between snapping pics and applauding. For posterity, he included a few shots of her fan club, pink shirts with Lydia's caricature on it. He then focused on her face, flushed with excitement and embarrassment. The three judges came out and shook her hand, offering congratulations.

Set up with a Lex-Tat official background, Aurelius waited for the contestants to get their official photos. He adjusted his camera settings between shots, not in a hurry. While less coordinated than a wedding, the convention was also less stressful and more entertaining.

He met many new contacts, and, on the whole, people acted with more kindness.

"I think we may know each other," Lydia accused, pointing at his shirt. "That looks familiar."

A bubble of pride gurgled in Aurelius's chest. "This old thing? I found it at a thrift store." Rat covered his mouth as he gave a loud, barking laugh. Catching her grin, he threw his arm across her shoulder and squeezed. "Judge's Choice? Aren't we Miss Fancy-Pants?"

"Stop," she cried and pinched his side.

He kissed the top of her head. "You deserve it. Congratulations."

Making a kissy-face, Rat threw his arms around Aurelius's neck. "Do I get some of that action? I was the one who suffered for hours."

Rubbing the man's head, Aurelius said, "Sure. Your wife's waiting. Let me grab these photos, and you can go play tonsil hockey all you want. You've my permission."

Out of the twenty shots he took, maybe he could submit two. Rat threw up bunny ears, peace signs, and stuck out his tongue. Lydia laughed, her eyes closed in every other picture. Worse case, he could join two of the best together in his editing software.

Later, as the convention whined down for the night, he and Lydia tidied up the shop's booth. Aurelius offered, hoping to gain points with Di, who was on the fence about him dating Lydia. He folded the t-shirts and sorted them into piles based on style and size. Behind him, Lydia wiped down all the equipment with a green antiseptic spray.

"Are you getting hungry?" she asked, tossing aside her used black nitrile gloves into a waste bin.

"Starved, actually."

She sidled up to him, her hip brushing his. "Miah's on a date tonight. Do you want to come over?"

Eying her, he said, "A date, huh? The IT guy finally asked her out?"

"No, she asked him." Lydia laid her hands on the top of his, stopping him from folding the last shirts. "Leave it. I'm hungry and want something bad for me."

Waggling his eyebrows, he grinned. "Are you insinuating I'm bad for you?"

"It's not an insinuation if it's true," stated Lydia as she ran her hand across his ticklish side.

Jumping, he pawed at her arm, too familiar with the game. "Don't do it."

"Do what?"

"I mean it, Lydia. Don't."

With a wicked smirk, she wiggled her fingers. "Go on, beg. It changes nothing."

He ran for his life.

About the Author

As a self-proclaimed biblio-phile and research geek, it's no wonder Jennie L. Morris writes romance and historical fiction with a flair for realism. Her love for learning led her to obtain degrees in Anthro-pology and Biology, which she often relies upon during writing. Coming from NE Ohio and raised on a small beef cattle farm, life was anything but ordinary growing up.

Jennie now resides in rural Kentucky, among the bluegrass and dazzling horse farms, with her amazing southern gentleman of a husband and their spoiled boxer pup Archie (Archibald Nubbintgon III). When she isn't reading or writing, she feeds her tea obsession or perfume addiction, letting the scents and flavors fuel her creative fires.

www.jennielmorris.com

https://linktr.ee/AuthorJennieLMorris

www.ingramcontent.com/pod-product-compliance
Lightning Source LLC
Chambersburg PA
CBHW071926120726
48001CB00005B/1883